INTRODUCTION

by Gary Carter

The New York Mets, the team I played for from 1985 to 1989, won the World Series in 1986. It was a highlight of my baseball career. But I remember how hard it was for us to win the fall classic. Our opponents, the Boston Red Sox, had won the first two games—at Shea Stadium, our home field!

We fought back, however, and took the next two games at Fenway Park, Boston's home field. In that fourth game, I hit two home runs. We lost the fifth game at Boston and headed home to Shea Stadium knowing we were one game away from being eliminated.

People still come up to me and ask about the pivotal sixth game of the 1986 World Series. The first nine innings ended in a tie, 3–3. But the Red Sox scored two runs in the top of the tenth inning to take a 5–3 lead. Then, our first two batters in the bottom of the tenth flied out. The Red Sox were one out away from winning the World Series.

Three straight Met singles followed, however, and we scored one run with them. That made the score 5–4. Mookie Wilson, an outfielder, was at the plate. Soon he had two strikes on him. The Red Sox were now just one strike away from becoming world champions.

But a wild pitch let in the tying run. And then Mookie hit a ground ball toward first base, a ball that went through the Red Sox fielder's legs as the winning run scored for us. We had won the sixth game, 6–5. And we went on to win the seventh and deciding game, 8–5.

I had had a very good World Series, collecting eight hits, two homers, and nine runs batted in. But I was not named the World Series MVP. That honor went to our third baseman, Ray Knight.

What did that mean?

To my mind, it meant that Ray came through for us when we needed him the most. For example, he hit only one home run in the Series, but it put us ahead to stay in the seventh game.

But the biggest single reason I think Ray was picked as the most valuable player was that he led by example. His great effort on the field and at the plate was an inspiration to all of us on the team. He set a standard to shoot for, and so we all tried to do better.

In this book, Robbie Belmont goes through a hard period of adjustment. It's his first year of college, of living away from home, and he struggles at the plate for the Redstone Colts, his college baseball team. But when the game is on the line as it is at the end of this book, Robbie sets the kind of example that inspires his whole team. It's not so much what he does, though that's important—it's how he leads.

Leadership made Ray Knight our MVP in 1986, and leadership is what separates Robbie Belmont from all others at the conclusion of this book. It is the one quality that can't be measured—but every winning organization, whether in baseball or outside of it, must have it somehow.

Chapter One

Robbie Belmont went into his catcher's stance and signaled for a fast ball. Eagle Wilson was pitching.

When Robbie had been a freshman at Riverton High School, Eagle Wilson had been the team's star pitcher. Now, Robbie was a freshman at Redstone University, and Eagle was the team's starting pitcher. It was a little like old times, with one exception.

Eagle Wilson hated Robbie's guts.

The fast ball burned in mean and low—too low! Robbie bunched his body in front of the ball's submarine path. The ball suddenly nicked the back edge of the plate, bouncing higher than it normally would. It bonged off Robbie's mask, jarring his head back. He hustled and picked up the deflected ball, his ears still ringing. There was no one on base, so there was no hurry. He tossed the ball back to Eagle, saying nothing.

He and Eagle talked to each other only when necessary. Robbie chattered with the other pitchers, but not with Eagle. He didn't have anything against Eagle. He just knew Eagle would not be helped by his chatter.

The reason Eagle had such a bad feeling toward Robbie was no secret. Eagle had dated Cynthia Wu, now a Redstone sophomore, for about five years. During that time, the two had many ups and downs. They'd break apart for a while, then get back together. Even now, Eagle didn't believe it was really over between them, although Cynthia said it was. Robbie was the one she was seeing now.

Eagle shook off Robbie's signal for a cross-seamed fast ball, a "lifter." Then Eagle shook off Robbie's signals for a "sailer" (a fast ball thrown with the seams) and an in-shooting "cutter" fast ball. Then he shook off the signals for a curve and a change-up. Robbie tried combining a couple of signals, calling for a change-up curve. But Eagle shook that off even more impatiently.

Robbie began again, signaling for the three types of fast balls—"lifter," "sailer," and "cutter." Eagle shook them off. Feeling anger well up inside him, Robbie put down two fingers again for the curve. This time, Eagle nodded. He would throw the curve.

While Eagle shook off all these signs, the batter had waited very calmly. He was Hank Green-grass, a sophomore center fielder.

Hank's father was Gus Greengrass, who had played five years in the major leagues as center fielder for the New York Titans. Gus Greengrass had been one of Robbie's childhood heroes. Gus's batting average for those five years had been .303. But his career had ended suddenly one game when he crashed into the center-field wall. Gus made the catch, but he injured his shoulder badly. After that, he couldn't throw or bat for power anymore and had to retire from the game. Robbie remembered how sad Gus looked when he announced his retirement on TV. He was still in his prime.

Hank Greengrass had the same confident way at the plate as his father. Eagle went into his wind-up. Hank went into his batting stance as calmly as he had been waiting. He looked strong at the plate and ready for the pitch.

The curve, like the fast ball before it, shot too low. Again, the pitch went into the dirt. Robbie stepped sideways like a crab and lowered his body in front of the curve gone awry. The spin of the pitch made it take a nasty bounce off the ground, but Robbie was right there. His catch-er's mitt closed around the ball.

"Nice pickup," Hank Greengrass said to Robbie.
"Thanks."

Robbie tossed the ball back to Eagle. He snatched it angrily out of the air.

"I hope Eagle can decide what to throw a little more quickly this time," said Hank. "I almost fell asleep before he threw that last pitch."

Robbie smiled, then cut it short before Eagle could see it. He started giving signals to Eagle again. Eagle shook off four straight. The Colts' manager, Frank Preston, called "Time." Coach Preston walked toward the mound and waved for Robbie to come out, too.

It was only the fourth day of practice for the Redstone University Colts. And it was Robbie's first time catching Eagle at the college level. Robbie knew he was in a close competition with last year's catcher, Wally Potenza.

Wally was Eagle's best friend. Last year, he had been the catcher who called the pitches that led to Eagle's eighteen wins and eight losses. Wally had caught Eagle in yesterday's practice game. Eagle did not shake off any of Wally's signs.

"Eagle," began Coach Preston, clearly annoyed, "I could have mowed the outfield between your pitches. Why are you shaking off so many?"

"Well, sir, I thought I'd get the batter nervous if I made him think I had that many pitches," said Eagle.

"What about the second time you shook off pitches?" the Colts' manager asked his starting pitcher.

7

"The catcher didn't give me the signal I wanted. He doesn't read me like Wally does."

"That's not the reason," said Robbie.

Frank and Eagle looked at him. No one said anything for a moment. Then the manager asked, "What is the reason, Robbie?"

"It's personal," said Robbie.

Eagle glared at Robbie.

"Leave your personal problems off the field, both of you," the coach said. "On the field, you play baseball. You hear me, Eagle?"

"Yes, sir, I do. But it's not personal. I don't know what the little hotshot means."

"Don't shake off any more pitches, Eagle," said Frank Preston sternly. "You're making it hard for your fielders to stay on their toes, and I want to see what kind of game Robbie calls. You understand?"

"I understand!" snapped Eagle.

"Watch your tone, Eagle," said Frank Preston. "The only people who have the right to pop off on this ball club are the coaches. Especially me."

"Sorry," said Eagle.

The coach walked off the field, and Robbie headed back behind the plate. The umpire was Jay Manning, assistant coach for the Colts. He was a young man, a graduate student at Redstone, studying sports medicine. Jay had played outfield for the Colts just three years ago. He was a cheerful person. Robbie liked him.

8

The fun came back into catching as Robbie gave Eagle the signal for a change-up curve. It was a great relief knowing Eagle wouldn't be shaking his signal off. Robbie had noticed that Hank started stepping as soon as Eagle released the ball. A change-up would catch Hank way in front of the pitch.

A slight look of disgust passed over Eagle's face as he saw Robbie's signal. He sighed, rolled his eyes up briefly, then went into his wind-up.

Sure enough, as Eagle released the ball, Hank started his stride. The dipsy-doodle curve floated peacefully under Hank's off-balance swing.

"Strike one!" called Jay Manning. Hank Greengrass, instead of getting mad at being fooled, was laughing.

"I'll say this much, Belmont," Hank said, "Wally Potenza would never have called a pitch like that!"

Robbie next signaled for a regular curve. Eagle again hesitated. Then he wound up and delivered.

It was a hanging curve, too high and too fat. Hank Greengrass had once more started his step too soon, but not as soon as on the last pitch. His smooth stroke cracked the pitch between the left and center fielders for a standup double.

"Nice call, freshman," Eagle shouted from the mound to Robbie.

"Lousy pitch, Wilson," Jay Manning called

back. "You hung that curve out to dry! Come on, don't blame your catcher."

Robbie didn't say anything. He thought Eagle might have hung the curve on purpose to make Robbie look bad. *Would Eagle go that far?* Robbie wondered.

Yes, he might, he answered himself.

As the practice game went on, Robbie's suspicions got stronger. Eagle didn't make it obvious, but it seemed he was getting hit a lot harder than usual by his own team. Robbie had sharp eyes. He knew when a pitch was slower or wilder than it normally was. Robbie also knew that Eagle, a control pitcher, did not hang that many curves or groove that many pitches. Eagle was a corner-nicking pitcher. So why was he throwing so many gopher balls down the middle of the plate?

Between innings, Eagle complained to Coach Preston that Robbie was calling bad pitches. The coach would listen silently for a while, then wave Eagle away.

In the seventh inning, Frank Preston brought Wally Potenza in to catch for Eagle. Robbie became the catcher for the other team. Immediately, Eagle Wilson was a changed pitcher. His curves broke low and nasty. His fast balls nicked the corners for called strikes. And Wally Potenza didn't have to make a single pickup on a bad pitch. Eagle needed only eight pitches to strike out the first two hitters. But the next batter wouldn't be so easy.

It was Robbie.

The Redstone freshman had hit Eagle well in the practice game the day before, getting two singles in four at-bats. But the first pitch Eagle threw to Robbie today was faster than any pitch Robbie had seen yesterday. It was faster than any pitch Eagle had thrown when Robbie was catching! The pitch was a cross-seamed fast ball, rising from ankle-high to knee-high as it came in. Robbie was tempted to swing, but he decided to take it. "Strike one!" yelled out Jay Manning.

"Nice pitch, Eagle!" Robbie called, smiling a little.

"Shut up, Belmont!" Wilson yelled back.

"Now that I know how fast you can throw it, I want to see the same speed when *I'm* catching for you!" Robbie called back.

"Shut *up*, Belmont!" Eagle said in a threatening tone of voice.

"Shut up, the two of you!" ordered Jay Manning from behind the plate.

Robbie stepped out of the box. He was angry that a teammate would actually hold back in a game, even if it was only a practice game. His blood running like fire through his veins, Robbie stepped back in the box. Eagle went into his wind-up and nearly fell sideways off the mound as he delivered. Crossfire fast ball!

11

The pitch started toward the high inside corner, then bent in at Robbie's head. Robbie was concentrating so intensely that he could actually see the ball spinning. He moved his head back just the barest bit. The pitch just missed his forehead and buzzed by for ball one. Eagle had meant to brush Robbie back, to put some fear into him.

Robbie was not rattled by the pitch in the slightest. And he felt he knew what the next pitch would be. Another crossfire, but this time a crossfire curve. Robbie had seen Eagle and Wally pull this sequence of pitches before. First came the inside crossfire fast ball, scaring the batter. Next came the curve, starting right for the batter, then dipping over for a strike. It worked on a lot of batters, especially those who hadn't seen it before.

Sure enough, Eagle went into his crossfire delivery again. The pitch came right at Robbie, then curved. It was exactly what he was expecting.

Robbie tracked the ball in calmly. Then he unloaded on it. The fat part of his bat crunched the ball. It rocketed on an almost straight line toward the left-field fence. As a line drive, it normally wouldn't go for a home run. But this was no normal line drive. It kept rising! The ball cleared the fence by a few inches—and was still rising when it crashed into the empty bleacher seats.

As Robbie rounded first to trot out the home run, he heard Hank Greengrass shout from the bench, "Way to scorch that thing, Belmont!" The other players on the team, from both sides, clapped and gave Robbie encouragement as he made the tour of the bases.

"Way to sock it, Robbie!"

"Some shot, Belmont!"

"Way to go, Robbo!" shouted Robbie's old friends, Brian Webster and Joshua Kenny. They had been equipment managers on Robbie's high-school team, the Riverton Tigers, and were the same for the Redstone Colts.

"That's the kind of hitting we were waiting to see from you," Coach Preston said to Robbie.

In fact, it was only the first home run Robbie had hit so far this year in a practice game. Frank Preston and the whole team were expecting a lot from Robbie this year. Even though he was just a freshman, his reputation preceded him. Several major-league teams had offered him bonuses to play pro ball. Catchers were in short supply in the majors, and Robbie was one of the hottest-hitting and best-fielding catching prospects in the nation.

But Robbie had turned down the offers because he wanted to go to college. He felt he could improve his baseball skills just as well in college as in the minors. Maybe his stay in the minors would be a lot shorter if he went into pro ball from college instead of from high school.

The home run Robbie had just hit in the practice game boosted his confidence. So far, he had been struggling at the plate. Every time he swung and missed or swung and hit an easy out, Robbie felt all eyes were on him. He was starting to wonder if he would ever get another long-ball hit. The homer came as a relief to him and, he thought, to Redstone's coaching staff.

Still, it was not going to be easy for Robbie to make Redstone's starting line-up, pro prospect or not. His hitting would have to improve and become more consistent.

And somehow, he had to find a way to work with Eagle Wilson.

Chapter Two

"Eagle called me again," Cynthia Wu said to Robbie.

They were sitting in Cynthia's dormitory room. Her roommate was at the library. Robbie and Cynthia had been doing homework together. Of course, with them that meant doing some homework and a lot of talking.

"When?" Robbie asked.

"Six o'clock this morning," Cynthia said with a sigh. "Someone down the hall said there was a call for me at the pay phone. So I put on my bathrobe, walked down the hall, and put the phone to my ear. It was Eagle. He said he had a dream about me."

"What kind of dream?"

"I didn't give him the chance to say. I told him we could be friends but not boyfriend and girlfriend. I also told him I didn't enjoy waking up at six o'clock to answer the phone if it wasn't an emergency."

"What did he say to that?"

"He said it was sort of an emergency. To him." Cynthia rolled her eyes as she said this. "I finally told him not to bother me anymore. Then I said good-bye and hung up. But I just know he'll call again. He always does. Eagle can be a real jerk, you know."

"I know," said Robbie. The fact that Eagle was hassling Cynthia made Robbie angrier than ever at him.

"What bothers me about all this," said Cynthia, peering out her window, "is that Eagle and I used to help each other out a lot. Five years is a long time to know someone. And yet, I feel I don't know him at all. Not now, anyway." Cynthia looked directly at Robbie. "I guess feelings change between people sometimes."

"Not mine," blurted Robbie. He surprised himself with his comment—and the next. "Not about you."

Cynthia reached over and squeezed his hand.

"I'm going to have a talk with Eagle," said Robbie. "Maybe *I* can get through to him."

"I think that would make things worse, Robbie," said Cynthia.

"Well, we have to figure out something!" said Robbie in frustration.

16

"I have to get this book read, Robbie. Stop talking so much."

"And I have to get this essay written, Cynthia. Please don't say any more interesting things."

Smiling, they both returned to their homework for a few minutes. Cynthia read five pages from a history book, taking a few notes. Robbie stared out Cynthia's open window. On his lap, his notebook was open to a blank page.

Robbie's major was communications. He was interested in possibly becoming a journalist or a sports announcer after his baseball career. This semester, he was taking a course called "Descriptive Writing." His assignment was to write a one-page description of an object. He hadn't thought of a topic yet, although he'd been "doing homework" with Cynthia for two hours already.

He kept coming up with the idea of describing Cynthia because his eyes kept wandering back to her. But she wasn't an object! Maybe he could write about the book that Cynthia was reading. But he really didn't want to describe that. As he stared out the window, Robbie thought, *Maybe I should describe the scene outside Cynthia's window. The campus green, the trees ... But that's not one object—that's a bunch of objects.* Frowning, he looked back at Cynthia again.

"Is that frown for me?"

"Oh, no, nothing like that," Robbie said quickly.

"I'm just having trouble coming up with an object to describe for this assignment."

"What about a baseball?" Cynthia suggested.

"Too hard to make interesting."

"What about your catcher's mask?"

"My face-saver. Concussion-preventer. See the world through iron bars. A little jail for my head."

"I thought you said it had to be a plain physical description."

"Right," said Robbie. "And the describer is not supposed to be included in the description."

"What does that mean?" asked Cynthia.

"It means I'm supposed to keep myself out of the description of the object," said Robbie.

"What about your bat?"

"Ah!" said Robbie. "That's it! That's it!"

He immediately began writing in his notebook: *My father gave me a baseball bat the Christmas before last.*

Robbie stared at the sentence for a while. Then he scratched it out—he wasn't supposed to use himself in the description. He didn't like how the scratched-out sentence looked on the page. Robbie turned his notebook to a new, clean page. It remained clean as he looked blankly at it another minute. Then he wrote "A Baseball Bat" at the top of the page. That seemed right. It looked good. He didn't scratch it out. But he didn't write anything under it, either.

He thought of his bat. That made him think about his hitting. And that bothered him so much that he couldn't think about writing.

"I don't know why I'm not hitting better," he said to Cynthia.

She looked up from her book. "I thought you said you hit a home run yesterday in practice."

"Yeah, but I'm not consistent. Today, I only had one single in four at-bats. I felt like a stranger up there at the plate. I don't know what I'm doing wrong."

"What does Coach Preston say?"

"He hasn't said anything specific yet. Just 'Good hit' the few times I get a good hit. His assistant, Jay Manning, says he doesn't see me doing anything wrong, but he'll keep looking. If I'm not doing anything wrong, why aren't I hitting?"

"Maybe you're doing something wrong that can't be seen, like not concentrating."

"It must be, because I'm not hitting that well even in batting practice!"

"Maybe it's college," said Cynthia. "I bet it's college."

Robbie nodded. College had been a roller coaster ride of highs and lows for him. His first year at Redstone University was two thirds over, and he was still not used to it.

Robbie liked being on his own, but he also missed his parents a lot. They each wrote him frequently. He rushed to his student mailbox every day hoping for a letter from them and from his friends at other schools.

Melinda Clark, who used to help Robbie with his math homework, was studying computer science at Whalen University. Ralph Butler, who once tried out for Robbie's high-school baseball team, was a track star at Lansley University. He was also majoring in business there. Other friends from high school occasionally dropped Robbie a line. He was always glad to hear from them.

Robbie found it very hard to keep track of all the things on his college schedule. Being able to spend so much time with Cynthia was great. But his studies demanded so much time that it was hard to relax. There were times when Robbie felt he was attending not RU but RCU—"Roller Coaster University."

His mind had never been stretched so much. It could do things now he never dreamed possible at the beginning of the school year. The first week of classes, he walked around like a man stunned, wondering how he was *ever* going to do all the reading required. The first semester, it seemed all he did was read, eat, and sleep—then read some more.

As the first semester rolled on, Robbie's mind buzzed with ideas and facts. Then, a funny thing started to happen. He found he could read much more in a shorter time than he could when the year began. His mind was stronger. Training his body did not always make him better at baseball. But training his mind always made him better at learning. Robbie realized his mind was something that could keep growing long after his body reached its peak.

And falling in love with Cynthia was another feature ride at "Roller Coaster University." How they talked! They talked about everything, all the time, anywhere, whenever they could. Robbie could say anything to her! Anything! And he wanted to tell her everything. She felt the same way. It was exciting.

Still, there were days when he couldn't see Cynthia for some reason or another. He knew it was corny, but he sometimes missed her so much he could hardly move! Also, it seemed they cared for each other so much that the slightest careless action or word could hurt the other's feelings. When that happened, it was awful. But then they'd talk and come to understand each other again.

The whole process could be *very* tiring at times. And it came on top of a demanding study load and a heavy baseball schedule. That was what Cynthia meant when she said, "It's college."

"Yeah," said Robbie. "I wouldn't be surprised if college was weighing me down in the batter's box. It weighs me down everywhere else—why not there, too?"

"You'll adjust," said Cynthia. "Just give your-

21

self time. It's only been a week of practice so far."

"I'm worried about being beaten out by Wally Potenza. I have to make every day count. And he's been hitting a little better than me in practice, although he doesn't have any home runs or stolen bases yet."

"I like Wally," said Cynthia in a sad tone of voice.

"Well, that's the thing," said Robbie. "I do, too. He treats me fair and doesn't go along with Eagle when Eagle trashes me. I like Wally's personality, too. Sort of quiet, but kind."

"Wally's smart, too," said Cynthia. "He's the only philosophy major I know at Redstone."

"I wonder if he tells Eagle to stop hassling you and me," said Robbie.

"Why don't you ask him?"

"Nah, I can't just ask him right out. I need to get to know him first."

"Well, get to know him! You're a communications major—so communicate! Seems to me two catchers should have no problem talking with each other, anyway."

"Oh, yeah? What about Eddie Mosely? Remember him?"

Eddie Mosely made life miserable for Robbie during his freshman year of baseball at Riverton High School. Each wanted to be the starting catcher.

"Yes, I do," answered Cynthia. "I admit Eddie was no day at the beach. But even *he* came around later on. Remember?"

Robbie nodded reluctantly. Cynthia had a way of showing him two sides to every question, every opinion. Sometimes it made him very uncomfortable, but he was always grateful in the end.

"Okay, okay, I'll talk to Wally."

"Good."

Suddenly, three heads popped into Cynthia's open dorm window on the first floor. Robbie jumped out of his chair, spilling his notebook onto the floor. The heads belonged to Joshua Kenny, Brian Webster, and Hank Greengrass.

"Did I hear Cynth say it was good that we dropped by to pick you two up for a pizza run?" Josh asked.

"We were talking about something else," said Cynthia sheepishly.

"Uh-huh," said Josh. "Well, I'm talking about pizza. With the works. Extra cheese, pepperoni, mushrooms, ground beef, green peppers, onions, sausage, and of course—"

"ANCHOVIES!" everyone else shouted in unison, completing Josh's mouth-watering list of toppings. Then they all laughed.

"No can do, guy," Robbie said finally. "I've got to finish this essay."

"Sure, Robbie," said Brian. "We all know finishing your essay is your main reason for being in this young lady's room."

Robbie, usually so quick with a comeback to his old friend Brian, just sat there grinning.

"Hmm, sure is quiet around here," said Hank Greengrass.

Everyone laughed, then Josh, Brian, and Hank said their good-byes. Robbie and Cynthia sat there looking at each other with little smiles on their faces. Then they returned to their work.

After an hour, Cynthia shut her book with a thump and said, "Finished! Beat you!"

Robbie was writing fast now in his notebook. It was a one-page assignment and he was in the middle of page two. Three sentences ago, he thought he had written the last sentence! But each time he finished his supposedly last sentence, another sentence about his bat came out. He was wondering if the one he was writing now would be his last sentence.

Robbie finished the sentence, then paused over the page. No more sentences came.

"Done," he said, closing his notebook. "First draft, anyway. I'll have to go over it again tomorrow morning."

Robbie had received a C on his first essay for this course. He could hardly believe all the things the teacher had found wrong with it! He wanted to be extra careful this time.

Cynthia's roommate, Dori, came in. She was a

mild-mannered architecture major who had gone out with Josh Kenny a few times last year. Cynthia and Dori got along okay, but they weren't close friends.

"There's a phone call for you, Cynthia," Dori said. "Hi, Robbie."

"Hi, Dori," Robbie said.

"Is it Eagle Wilson?" asked Cynthia.

"Well, he wouldn't say who he was, so it's probably Eagle. It didn't sound like him, but he might have been disguising his voice. Let me go back and ask who it is again. If he won't say, I'll say you don't want to talk then."

"Thanks, Dori," said Cynthia. "I really appreciate it."

"Glad to help, Cynthia." Dori walked out of the room and back to the pay phone in the hall. Robbie and Cynthia took the opportunity to kiss each other good night. Dori returned.

"It was Eagle Wilson, and he said, 'Just tell her and the gentleman she's with that life is not as easy as they think.' "

"He doesn't know how easy we think life is," said Cynthia in a quiet voice.

Exactly what Robbie had been thinking.

Robbie said his good nights and left. He walked across the campus green in the warm spring night. He heard the sounds of students laughing and talking as he passed various dorms. Music could be heard from many rooms. Sometimes the songs competed with each other.

Robbie thought of his essay, and then he started thinking of his bat. Writing the description had made him eager to get his hands on it at practice tomorrow.

All the while, the memory of Cynthia glowed warmly in him.

Chapter Three

The competition between Robbie Belmont and Wally Potenza for the starting catcher's position lasted all preseason. It was nip and tuck all the way. One day, Robbie would suddenly come alive at the plate, getting a number of extra-base hits. But another day, it would be Wally who hit the long ball and Robbie who hit weakly. Some days, they both hit well; other days, both hit badly. The batting average for each came to a little under .300.

This was a good batting average, but it seemed poor to Robbie. There was a period during his last year of high school when Robbie hit at a .600 clip! But college pitching, even during the preseason, was at least twice as good as high-school pitching. Robbie was now competing with players whose talents were more like his own. In high school, he was a one-in-a-million star. Now he seemed to be just one among many. Robbie was good, but he wasn't showing "greatness" yet. Since he wasn't used to being "only pretty good," it made him feel worse!

Eagle Wilson didn't help him any, either. Robbie always played his best when he enjoyed playing, when he batted or fielded with the zest he had felt as a child learning the game. But Eagle's gloomy attitude and anger toward him turned baseball into a chore for Robbie. The harmony that made a great team was missing. Bad feelings between the pitcher and catcher made a team seem rotten at its core!

Frank Preston and Jay Manning knew what was going on and watched Eagle carefully. Coach Preston bawled Eagle out a number of times for his bad attitude and poor team spirit. When Eagle threw two straight gopher balls to Wally Potenza in one practice game, Coach Franklin yanked the pitcher.

The problem was, however, that Eagle was the Colts' best pitcher by far. No other pitcher approached him in talent. There was a sophomore hurler named Clem Goodall. Clem threw hard and had a promising future. But he was still too inconsistent. He was not experienced enough to be the Colts' main starter.

When Wally Potenza was catching for Eagle, the pitcher's attitude seemed to brighten a lot. Eagle then would go out of his way to look cheerful. And he'd be full of pep on the bench. But it was forced cheer, and everyone on the team knew it. The players would give each other wry looks when Eagle would throw his fist in the air and say "Way to go, Wally" after striking someone out. When Wally got a hit, Eagle would leap off the bench clapping too hard and yelling too long.

Team morale was bad. This bothered Robbie more than anything. Because he was striving to be the team's starting catcher, team spirit concerned him greatly. He spent a lot of time thinking about what he might do to help bring the Colts closer together. He talked with Cynthia about the problem from many different angles. And he talked about it with Brian and Joshua.

Obviously, Eagle was the heart of the problem. Robbie wasn't sure how to deal with him, but a catcher had to know how to deal with his pitcher! When Eagle had a temper tantrum, Robbie tried to keep his own temper. He didn't want to pour fuel on Eagle's fire. Robbie wanted to play the best team baseball he could.

As opening day got closer, Frank Preston bore down on Eagle harder and harder. The coach yelled at him in practice. "Show me what you've got, Eagle! I want to see your best stuff!"

During an inning changeover, Robbie accidentally overheard the coach speak to Eagle near the dugout. "If I ever catch you grooving the

29

ball or muffing on purpose, Eagle, I promise you the best seat in the house—the bench. And you'll stay there until your butt turns to stone. You've got the talent. But talent isn't enough. Desire and this"—the coach was pointing to his head—"make the difference."

Eagle knew Coach Preston meant what he said. The next time Wally Potenza faced him at the plate, Eagle whiffed him on five pitches. Eagle's fielding also improved immediately. He actually dived at and speared a line drive that looked like a sure hit. His teammates applauded as he brushed the dirt from his clothes. But Eagle still didn't talk with Robbie and glared at him constantly. That much stayed the same.

Everyone on the team knew Eagle had a good shot at pro ball. If he had the great season expected of him this year, he seemed sure to become a high draft pick. But first things were first—Eagle wanted to win the opening game of the season. Even then, there would be scouts scattered in the stands.

When he got a chance to pitch against Robbie in practice, Eagle reached back for a little extra. On one at-bat a few days before opening day, Eagle threw Robbie faster fast balls and sharper-breaking curve balls than he'd thrown to anyone ever!

"Nice pitch!" Robbie called from the batter's

box to Eagle on the mound after a snapping slider nicked the corner for strike two.

Eagle's face remained stony. He caught Wally Potenza's return throw and turned his back on Robbie.

"He should throw that way against every batter, not just you, Robbie," said Wally Potenza in the catcher's box.

"I agree," said Robbie.

The next fast ball burned in low and inside. It was too close to let pass. Robbie swung and hit the ball on the thin part of the bat. There was a loud crack. The bat had shattered in two, sending the ball into shallow center field. The heavier part of the bat hurtled toward the left of the mound as Robbie ran for first base.

The ball looked as if it might drop between the infielder and outfielder for a single, or Texas leaguer. But Hank Greengrass did a long belly-slide and snagged it for a sensational catch.

While the players were cheering Hank's play, Robbie headed back to the plate. Wally Potenza had retrieved the heavier part of the bat from aside the mound and was now holding both pieces.

"I know what you must be feeling," said Wally, handing the pieces over to Robbie. "I broke my bat in almost the same spot last year. I felt lost without it. Funny how a bat can become a part of you, something you think you can't get along

without. But you can, and you will. You'll find another. I did."

Robbie knew Wally was trying to make the loss easier on him. But Robbie also knew no two bats were made exactly alike, and that fact made him sadder than ever. He had loved the bat, with its black and white marbled barrel and the handle so perfect for his hands. The essay he had written about it a few weeks ago had earned Robbie his first B. His hitting had begun to get better, in fact, after the essay!

This was the bat that had struck so many power hits, his good friend away from home, his special tool! And now he was in a hot hitting contest with Wally Potenza for the starting catcher's spot. The bat was the only thing that had been giving him confidence lately. It was the bat his father had given him as a Christmas present two years ago.

After practice, Robbie walked out of the locker room with Hank Greengrass. Wally Potenza caught up with them. "Hey, let me give you guys a lift home."

Wally was one of the few players who had a car. Robbie was exhausted from a hard test he had taken that morning and the hard, bat-breaking practice. He gladly accepted the ride, and so did Hank.

Wally didn't say anything for the first part of the ride. Hank and Robbie talked about batting, as they often did. Hank told Robbie, "You'll start hitting again, Robbie. I know it." Hank's words encouraged Robbie a lot because Hank was hitting hotter than a house on fire these days. Wally listened calmly to their talk. He didn't seem to mind at all that his catching rival was getting batting advice. In fact, he seemed to approve of it.

Wally turned his car into a shopping mall and drove up to a sporting goods store. He parked and turned to Robbie with a smile.

"Robbie," he said, "Ol' Wally is going to buy you a present. Come on."

They all went into the store. Hank was just as curious as Robbie. Wally walked directly to the section that sold bats.

"Pick your favorite, Rob. It's on me," said Wally. "I want my worthy rival to like his bat as much as I like mine. If I'm going to beat you out, I don't want any unfair advantage!"

Hank Greengrass applauded. "All right, Wally! Good man!" he said.

Robbie laughed and said, "I thank you, worthy opponent." He gave Wally a little bow. Now Wally laughed.

Robbie tried out various bats for about fifteen minutes. One aluminum bat attracted him. Every player on the team used an aluminum bat but Robbie. Aluminum bats seemed livelier than wooden bats. But since they weren't allowed in the majors, Robbie didn't want to get used to one! He also disliked the metallic clang an aluminum bat made when hitting a baseball. The solid crack of good wood meeting the ball would always be the best music to Robbie's ears.

He finally settled happily on a thirty-four-inch, plain wooden bat that felt just right in his hands. Wally paid for it. Hank picked up a New York Titans sweat shirt to send to his father.

Wally dropped Hank off, then drove to Robbie's dorm. Robbie didn't get right out. He wanted to talk a little with Wally about Eagle, and he sensed Wally did, too.

"Any suggestion for Cynthia and me about Eagle?" Robbie asked.

"Well," said Wally, "I tell him not to bother you two, but he doesn't listen to me about that. To tell you the truth, I'm sorry about the whole thing. It's really cruel to Cynthia, and it's bad for the team when he takes it out on you. I have some sympathy for him, of course. He is my friend, and he does miss Cynthia a lot. But he's going too far. He's trying to prove something that doesn't need proving. He hates the idea that he failed with Cynthia. Success means more to him than the people around him. So he lives in his own world a lot. That doesn't help him with Cynthia, and it hurts his concentration as a pitcher."

"So how should I deal with him?" Robbie asked Wally. "Is there any hope of snapping him out of it?"

"We probably shouldn't expect miracles overnight," Wally said, looking into the darkening sky. "And I think the way you've been dealing with him so far is pretty good. You keep an even temper, but you don't back down, either."

"I'd sure like to get him out of that bad mood he's in."

"If we could somehow make it more interesting in the real world for him, that would help, I bet!"

"What does he like?" Robbie asked. "Besides succeeding with Cynthia?"

"He likes pitching," replied Wally. "He wants to be known as a great pitcher."

Both Wally and Robbie fell silent, thinking.

"I know what Eagle would like!" said Robbie. "He'd like a perfect game!" Though he didn't know why, Robbie felt sure of it.

"You're right," said Wally, laughing and shaking his head. "He'd love to be known as the King of the Perfect Game!"

"We could fire him up to go for it! We can get him to go for the perfect game record!"

"What is the record, anyway?" asked Wally.

"Well, as far as I know, only eight perfect games have ever been thrown in Division One NCAA baseball. And they were all by different pitchers."

"So no one pitcher has ever pitched two perfect games at the Division One level."

"Right."

36

"Well, then, that's what we'll have Eagle shoot for—two perfect games. He has an ego big enough to think he can do it, too."

"He also has the control. Eagle can pinpoint the ball better than anyone I've ever caught. Imagine—no men on base, twenty-seven straight outs, done *twice* in a season. That should make the scouts' heads swim."

"And Eagle's."

" 'Pitcher Perfect,' " said Robbie. "I can see the headline in the school newspaper now."

"School newspaper? Heck, ol' Eagle might get his face plastered on the cover of *Sports Illustrated* for two perfect games! It's enough to make me think of canceling my subscription!"

Both boys laughed.

"I've got to get back," said Wally after a moment of quiet. "I still have some booking to do before tomorrow."

"Me, too," said Robbie. He opened the car door and stepped out.

"Forgetting something, guy?"

"Oh, right." Robbie looked a little embarrassed as he reached in for the bat Wally had bought him. "Sorry. Guess my mind was on Eagle."

"One final piece of advice, Robbie," said Wally. "Let Eagle worry about Eagle. He does a better job than any of us. Know what I mean?" Wally gave Robbie a wink.

"Yeah, Wally, I think I do," answered Robbie

with a laugh. "I think I do. Thanks for the talk—and the new bat."

"No problem. We catchers have to stick together."

As Wally headed off in his car, Robbie tried to remember where he had heard that last comment before. *Eddie Trent!* thought Robbie. The star catcher for the New York Titans had said the same thing to Robbie during his first year of high-school ball.

The next day at practice, Robbie and Wally approached Eagle together. They both told him they wanted him to shoot for a perfect game every time he pitched. Eagle scoffed at the idea at first, but Robbie saw he was interested. The seed had been planted.

The last few practices found Robbie and Wally still in a tight contest. No one knew whom Frank Preston would choose. Preston himself didn't know.

Robbie's new bat worked just as well as his old bat. He was still hitting only about once every three at-bats, as was Wally. But on the last day, Robbie's catching finally won out. He had learned a lot about all the Colt batters by now. He always had a terrific memory for what batters liked and didn't like. And on the Friday before the Saturday opener, Eagle allowed three hits and two walks when Wally caught, but got out sixteen straight batters when Robbie caught!

After practice, Coach Preston called Wally and Robbie into his office. "Gentlemen," he began, "you've both been giving a great effort, and I thank you. We'll be starting with Robbie tomorrow. Wally, you're a fine catcher, and you've done the Colts a lot of good, this year and last."

"Thanks, Coach," Wally said, sounding more than a little disappointed. "I admit Eagle pitched better when Robbie was catching today."

"And that was mostly Eagle's doing, not Robbie's, I know," said the manager. "But Robbie's speed on the base paths tipped the scales in his favor."

"It's these darn flat feet of mine!" said Wally.

Coach Preston went over and patted Wally on the back. "I have something else in mind for you, Wally, if you're up to the task."

"Coach?"

"Ever think about playing right field?"

"But Charlie Diskin has that spot nailed down."

"I'm not saying I'm going to give the spot to you now," said Frank Preston cautiously. "But I'd like to give you a shot at it. You're a better hitter than Charlie. And you have a real head for the game, something we could use more of out there. Think about it, okay?"

"Sure, Coach. Okay."

"Good." Frank Preston now looked at Robbie. "Don't let me down, Robbie. I know you've had some problems with Eagle. Work them out. Get him to trust you. Get him to pitch the way I know he can."

"I'll be the best catcher Eagle can have," said Robbie.

"And if you aren't," said Wally with a half-serious laugh, "I will."

Chapter Four

Eagle found out in the locker room before the opening game that Robbie was the starting catcher. Coach Preston read off the starting line-up and batting order. Robbie's name was announced sixth. A groan escaped from Eagle's mouth when he heard it.

"Chill out, Eagle," Robbie called to his pitcher in a friendly voice. "You won't be groaning that I'm behind the plate after we start mowing down every single batter!" The other players clapped at the idea.

The starting line-up was as follows:

    (1) Oscar Gonzales, SS
    (2) Hank Greengrass, CF
    (3) Charlie Diskin, RF
    (4) Jeff Streets, 1B

(5) Lou Ranger, LF

(6) Robbie Belmont, C

(7) Tip Tyree, 3B

(8) Sidney Fisher, 2B

(9) Eagle Wilson, P

After Coach Preston finished announcing the line-up, the team burst from the locker room, revved up.

The Colts were playing at home in Redstone Stadium, a solid, handsome ballpark, newly painted in the Colts' colors of red and brown. About two thousand fans roared and cheered when the Colts ran onto the field. Robbie had heard louder crowds before, but it sounded great just the same.

Robbie's parents had driven up from Riverton for the game. Robbie could make out his mother's strong, throaty voice in the crowd. Ellen Belmont was a physical therapist and an athlete in her own right, primarily a swimmer. Robbie saw his father standing and clapping, with the usual thoughtful look on his face. St. Simon Belmont taught English at the state university close to Riverton, Fuller University. The year before, Simon had had a severe eye problem, but it had cleared up after a while. There had been no signs of the problem returning since then.

Robbie hit well in batting practice and looked sharp during the infield warm-up. He felt full of confidence when he went to warm up Eagle, so Eagle's bad mood didn't bother him.

Eagle Wilson had his own way of warming up, and the catcher was only a tiny part of it. Eagle went into some sort of invisible shell. He acted more in his own world than ever. He started by throwing medium fast balls through all the various parts of the strike zone. He threw three pitches each place: down the middle, low outside corner, high outside corner, high inside corner, low inside corner, and middle inside and outside corners.

Then he threw three balls each for places *outside* the strike zone: very tight inside, low but a bit outside, and high inside and outside. Eagle was one of the few pitchers Robbie had ever caught who worked on proper placement of fishballs. These were pitches not in the strike zone but tempting enough to make the batter "fish" for the ball. Most strikeouts came on fishballs thrown with two strikes. With two strikes on him, the batter has to protect the plate and will swing at anything close. Eagle liked to give a batter in the hole bad pitches to "fish" for.

Then Eagle started throwing harder. He worked on his three different types of fast ball. He threw them through the same points in and out of the strike zone as before. Then he did the same with his curve, change-up, and crossfire. Eagle ended his warm-up by firing three full-speed fast balls

43

down the middle. Then he just walked away toward the dugout, without waiting for Robbie. Robbie jogged to catch up with him.

"Way to pitch, Eagle. You put the ball just where you wanted it except for eight times."

"Six times, Belmont!" the pitcher said suddenly, turning to Robbie.

Robbie grinned. "Well, two were close calls, but I'll go along with six." Robbie was sure Eagle almost smiled. They were both pleased at how closely the other was counting. And Eagle's placement today was looking great.

A group from the Redstone Glee Club sang the national anthem. They called themselves the Redstone Coltones, and they always got the whole stadium singing along. Cynthia Wu was a Coltone. Robbie loved watching her sing in front of the stadium crowd. But he also noticed Eagle watching her and looking sadder than a basset hound.

The song ended, and the umpire yelled, "Play ball!" Robbie's college baseball career was about to begin.

Their opponents this game were the Crimson College Sultans. Crimson was not a very large school. But they had beaten the Colts last year, mostly because of a center fielder they had who was back again this year: Jack McKay. McKay had smacked two homers and a double against Eagle Wilson last year, driving in five runs. The Sultans had won, 5–4. The other Sultans were not as fearsome, but they were well disciplined. The Sultan manager drove them hard and drilled them well in the basics.

Robbie thought Eagle's first pitch, a rising fast ball, hit the high outside corner nicely. The umpire didn't. The next two pitches missed the inside corner by a hair. The count was three balls and no strikes. *Doesn't look too promising*, Robbie thought. But Eagle's next two pitches were strikes, one down the middle, the other across the knees. The umpire had a "low" strike zone, and Eagle was adjusting nicely.

The batter had taken five straight pitches. Robbie knew the scouting report on this batter. He took a lot of pitches and drew a lot of walks. He couldn't hit a curve, but Robbie didn't want to call for the curve with the count 3–2. But he did call for the sailing fast ball, which sailed away like a curve from a right-handed hitter. Eagle snapped off a perfect sailer, and the batter swung and missed for strike three.

Robbie threw the ball to the Colts' first baseman, Jeff Streets, to start the infield throwing the ball around.

"Way to mow 'em down, Eagle!"

"Here we go! Here we go!"

"Keep it up, Eags! Keep right on going!"

The next batter grounded out to Jeff Streets at first base. The following batter hit a two-strike pitch that Eagle had purposely thrown a shade

45

inside. It dribbled two yards in front of the plate. Robbie pounced on the ball, scooping it up with glove and bare hand. He fired a perfect strike to Streets, nipping the runner by an inch for the third out.

The Colts also went down one-two-three in the bottom half of the first inning. The first batter Eagle had to face in the top of the second was Jack McKay. "Blackjack" McKay, as he was known by his friends and fans, was tall and stocky—a rare combination.

"What size is that bat?" Robbie asked McKay.

"Forty inches."

That was a lot bigger than Robbie's thirty-four-inch bat! McKay had slicked-back hair under his red and white hat. He was smiling at the weak sound the handful of Crimson fans made in Redstone Stadium.

Robbie had studied the scouting report on the Sultans very carefully. McKay could hit good *and* bad pitches, both with power. Wally Potenza had told Robbie that McKay's huge bat seemed to have a magnet for the ball, no matter how it came in. His wrist snap was so quick he could take a longer look at the incoming ball. Since he didn't step early, no change-up fooled him.

It sounded to Robbie like McKay would swing at almost anything. He trotted out to talk with Eagle.

"Let's try throwing him very bad pitches at

first, Eagle. He swings at first pitches. Start out with a sailer that goes about two feet wide of the plate. I don't want to hold my target there, but put it there, okay?"

"Are you out of your mind, Belmont? Throw a real bad ball on purpose?"

"Make it look tempting, but make it almost impossible to hit cleanly."

"Forget it. I've thrown to this guy before. You haven't. We'll just work him inside-outside and hope for the best."

"That's what you did last year. He hit three for four."

"This year—"

"This year," interrupted Robbie, "he'll go zero for three!" Robbie turned around before Eagle could reply, and jogged back to the catcher's box.

Robbie gave the signal for the sailer fast ball and put up a normal down-the-middle target. As Eagle went into his wind-up, Robbie could see that McKay was eager to swing.

The fast ball started out looking a shade out-side, in reach of McKay's extra-long bat. The overeager slugger started going for it. Then the ball started sailing *way* outside. Still, McKay's long aluminum bat kept tracking the ball like the magnet Wally had mentioned. The ball sailed even farther outside, and McKay reached way over and took a mighty whack at it.

He hit it off the end of his bat, putting an incredible spin on the ball. Robbie could see the weak pop-up curve in midair. It was looping and bending over Jeff Streets, who was backing up as fast as he could. Suddenly, Jeff turned and dived—and caught the ball in his bare hand! As he crashed to the ground, the ball jiggled up from his hand. He grabbed it, bobbling it three more times. The ball still had not touched the ground. Finally, he let the last bobble fall into his glove. There it settled for the putout!

The roar of the crowd had been rising and falling with each bobble. Now it broke into a huge sigh of relief and a standing ovation.

The crowd remained on its feet as Eagle struck out the next two batters. Six up, six down!

In the Colts' turn at bat, cleanup hitter Jeff Streets flied out to left field. Next up was Lou Ranger, Redstone's left fielder. It was natural that Lou's nickname was the "Lone Ranger," especially since he was a lone wolf kind of guy. When Lou's name was announced, the Redstone musicians in the stands played the "William Tell Overture." It was the theme of the *Lone Ranger* TV show many years ago.

Lou smashed a line drive to center that McKay made a nice catch on. There were two outs and no men on base when Robbie came to bat for the first time.

The Sultan pitcher, according to Redstone's

scouting report, was able but nothing special. Robbie looked to Jay Manning, who was coaching at first base, for the signal. Jay was giving him the "take" sign.

The first pitch was a humming fast ball for a strike. It reminded Robbie again of the difference between high-school ball and college ball. This "able" college pitcher threw faster than most of the best high-school pitchers Robbie had faced!

Robbie saw an "able" curve next. Again, the pitch impressed him. But he followed it clearly and walloped it on the fat of his bat into center field. The crowd groaned—it was hit right at the center fielder! McKay took only one step to his right and waited for the scorching line drive to smack into his mitt for the third out.

"Too bad, Robbie!"

"Great wood, kid. Tough luck!"

"Hit solidly but right at him."

Brian Webster brought Robbie's catching equipment to him. Robbie put it on outside the catcher's box rather than in the dugout. Wally Potenza warmed Eagle up while Robbie buckled up.

"Eagle's looking good, Wally!" Robbie called to him.

"Real good!" Wally said as he walked over to Robbie.

"I don't know how long it can last, but it's

great while it does!" said Robbie. He had his equipment on now.

"He's all yours. Good luck," said Wally. Then Wally called out to Eagle, "See you in the dugout three batters from now, dude!" Wally took his place in the dugout.

Eagle kept getting the batters out, one right after another. He was putting the ball *exactly* where he wanted, and Robbie was calling the right pitches. The Colts' fielding was superb. Lou Ranger's running catch of a liner down the left-field line in the fourth inning robbed the Sultan batter of a sure triple. And Robbie tumbled into the stands to nab a McKay foul ball in the sixth inning.

With two outs in the top of the seventh, the Colts' shortstop, Oscar Gonzales, backhanded a ball hit deep in the hole. Oscar jumped while still going toward the third-base line, and he threw the ball while moving away from first. Still, his throw was strong enough to nip the runner. That made seven innings of a perfect game! Two more innings left—six batters! The crowd was on its feet every pitch Eagle threw.

"Think he'll do it?" Robbie asked Hank Greengrass in the dugout during the Colts' turn at bat.

"Shhh," whispered Hank. "It's supposed to be bad luck to talk about it before it's over."

The other Colt players in the dugout jumped

to their feet at the sound of ball meeting bat. Jeff Streets had just cracked a single up the middle.

"We need a run, Robbie," Brian said. Robbie was on deck. He picked out the bat Wally had bought for him and walked to the on-deck circle.

Like the Sultans, the Colts hadn't scored yet. They were getting hits but not enough to bring any runners home.

Crimson College's pitcher walked Lou Ranger on six pitches. There were now two men on and no outs.

Robbie came to the plate. He had been at bat three times in this game and had yet to get a hit.

High time I did something with this new bat of mine, thought Robbie, digging in.

Chapter Five

So far, Robbie had lined out to center, flied out to left, and grounded out to third. The husky Sultan pitcher did not seem to be tiring.

Robbie knew he could hit him. For the first time at the plate this game, Robbie felt like a hitter up there. Redstone needed a run so Eagle wouldn't have to pitch more than nine innings. As far as Robbie was concerned, it was his job to get that run.

The Colts' catcher worked the count to 2–2. Then, an off-speed curve came toward him. It was low and inside, Robbie's favorite hitting spot. He whipped the new bat around, connecting on the fat of the bat. The ball rose high into deep left field. The only question in Robbie's mind as he ran toward first base was whether it'd be a double or a homer.

Another two feet higher, and the ball would

have gone over for a home run. But it hit the top part of the fence and caromed sharply backward. By the time the Sultan left fielder could gather it in and throw it to the infield, Jeff Streets and Lou Ranger had crossed the plate. And Robbie was on second base with a standup double. Redstone's fans went wild, whooping and clapping and waving pennants. The Colts were on the scoreboard!

The game went into the top of the ninth inning with Redstone ahead, 2–0. Eagle Wilson was just three batters away from a perfect game. Eagle, with a little help from his friends, had retired twenty-four straight batters. The seventh, eighth, and ninth hitters in the Sultans' order were slated to bat. Probably, the eighth and ninth batters would be pinch hitters.

The first batter in the ninth inning, the small Sultan second baseman, bunted Eagle's first pitch down the first-base line and tried to leg it out. Eagle slipped while running after the bunt and fell on his face. But Jeff Streets rushed in, nabbed the ball, wheeled, stretched, and tagged the heel of the runner just as he passed. One breathtaking out.

The crowd was clapping and stamping their feet in rhythm now. The next batter, a pinch hitter, was of medium build. He ran the count to 2–2, then fouled off four straight pitches. Eagle then threw one barely outside, which the hitter dared to let pass. The count was now 3–2. The batter then fouled off three more pitches in a row! The crowd groaned loudly with each foul. The tension in the stadium was electric.

Eagle was taking it well. He seemed determined to do his best. But the pressure was also so heavy it could easily throw him off. Eagle had managed to deliver seven out of the last eight pitches in the strike zone, despite the almost unbearable pressure. Robbie knew that the slightest little tinge of fear at the moment Eagle was throwing could make the ball go off course.

Robbie thought about calling time and going out to talk with Eagle. But Robbie decided against it. Eagle had been coming through fine, and Robbie didn't want to risk breaking that rhythm.

The Redstone catcher was a little at a loss as to what pitch to call against this Sultan pinch hitter. All the scouting report had said was that he didn't like high strikes. The pinch hitter was last year's leadoff batter for Crimson College. He wasn't starting in this game because of a pulled thigh muscle.

Robbie signaled for a rising fast ball, wanting a high strike to get this batter out. Eagle delivered it exactly on target, as he had been doing all game. The batter swung and ticked under the ball, looping a dinky pop-up a few yards to Robbie's left. Robbie flung off his mask and lunged toward it. The ball was falling softly. Robbie stretched as far as he could.

The ball fluffed down, hit the tip of Robbie's mitt, and plopped to the ground. The entire stadium groaned in disappointment. It had not been an error—the ball had been too far out of reach. Still, everyone had wanted the ball caught!

Eagle threw his glove onto the mound in disgust. It was the first time he had shown such a bad temper all game. Oscar Gonzales ran in from shortstop, picked up Eagle's glove, dusted it off, and handed it to him. Oscar said a few words to Eagle, who nodded and calmed down. Then Oscar called in to Robbie, "Nice try, Robbie! Here we go now! Get this one! One pitch at a time! Hum-babe! Hum-babe!"

Robbie had never been sure what "hum-babe" meant, but he had heard the word on baseball fields all his life. Whatever it meant, he was glad to hear it now.

The batter hit the next sinking cutter fast ball to Oscar at shortstop on two nice clean hops. Robbie ran down to first to back up the play in case of a wild throw. Oscar's throw was dead on. The crowd roared. Only one more out, and Eagle would become the ninth player in NCAA Division One history to pitch a perfect game!

The next batter, another pinch hitter, was a large freshman. He looked like a born slugger. There was no scouting report on him, but Robbie had watched him hit during batting practice. He was the kind of batter who swung for the fences each time, but didn't connect that often. When he did connect, it sometimes went for home-run distance.

Eagle handcuffed him with two cutter fast balls on the inside corner for two straight swinging strikes. The fans were not only on their feet now, but many were also jumping up and down calling for the final strike! Eagle looked confident. He was two strikes ahead of an inexperienced batter. Robbie called for a sailer fast ball. He wanted it to hop in the direction opposite from the first two cutters.

The batter was set up for the cutter, having seen two straight. The out-breaking hop on the sailer fast ball surprised him. He started to back away, expecting the ball to cut inward. As the ball sailed away from him, he took a feeble swing and ticked it slowly toward the second baseman.

Surprised he had hit the ball, the batter hesitated before running toward first. Then he slipped slightly because he tried to run too fast at the start. Robbie was already running down the first-base side to back up the throw as usual.

The slow-hit ball was rolling right between three Colt players. Second baseman Sidney Fisher ran in for it, Eagle Wilson darted sideways for it, and Jeff Streets charged it from first base. No one was covering first base for the throw!

Sprinting to the first base in full catching gear, Robbie tried to go even faster. He was only a step ahead of the large, lumbering Sultan runner. But the runner, after his faulty start, was now catching up to Robbie, inch by inch. The three Colt fielders arrived at the ball at almost the exact same time. But it was Eagle who picked up the slow roller. As Eagle straightened to throw, Robbie was only a foot ahead of the runner. They were in a race for the first-base bag just a few yards away.

Eagle seemed surprised to find no one covering first. He even took a split second to look in disgust at his first and second basemen for not being there. Then he sidearmed a hard, short throw to the bag.

Robbie's foot hit the bag just as the ball hit his glove. The next instant, Crimson College's pinch hitter piled into him. They both tumbled head over heels. The umpire loomed over Robbie, looking to see if Robbie had held on to the ball. Robbie was a little dazed lying on the ground. He didn't know himself if he was still holding the ball. He looked in his mitt. It was still there!

"OUT!" called the umpire, throwing his right thumb up grandly in the air. Redstone fans swarmed the infield. "Perfect game!" they all shouted. "Perfect game!"

Colt players ran toward Eagle and mobbed him. In a second, he was lifted onto their shoulders and riding high. The Colts paraded Eagle before the cheering fans. Eagle looked happier than Robbie had seen him for months. The "perfect" pitcher was doffing his hat again and again, as if it were something he was used to doing.

Robbie had slowly lifted himself from the ground. Then he found himself looking into the eyes of the base runner who had just tumbled into him. "Great play, Belmont," the Sultan pinch hitter said. "I thought I had first base free and clear when I saw all three fielders go after the ball. I forgot about you."

"Thanks," said Robbie. "Good game." The two shook hands. A few other Sultans came over to them, watching the other Colts carry Eagle around the field.

"Don't you want to join your teammates?" the Sultan pitcher asked Robbie.

"Well, sure, sooner or later. Later, I guess. Hey, you pitched a great game," Robbie told him. They shook hands.

Robbie shook hands with a number of Sultan players before the ovation for Eagle finally faded. Then both teams mingled, shaking hands.

After that, the two teams went their different ways. Eagle came up to Robbie angrily as they entered the tunnel that led from the dugout to the locker room. "What were you doing shaking hands with the Sultans while everyone else was carrying me around? Was that your way of putting me down?"

Robbie couldn't believe it. Eagle had just pitched a perfect game and he still found something to complain about. Robbie had called the game, drove in the winning runs, and made a great game-saving play to end the contest. Now Eagle was harping on Robbie's "post-game" performance!

"Eagle," said Robbie with a wry smile, "don't blow your perfect game by turning into a perfect idiot. You want some reporter or scout to overhear you bawling out your catcher for not kissing your spikes after the game?"

In fact, a reporter from Redstone's campus newspaper was walking up to Eagle right at that moment. Eagle's angry expression turned into a broad Hollywood smile the moment the reporter aimed his camera at him.

Robbie laughed and walked away from the scene. Wally Potenza joined him on the walk to the locker room.

"Well, I hate to say this, chum," Wally said, "but you looked kind of permanent behind the plate today."

"Thanks, Wally. What a game, eh? Perfect game, just as we talked about!"

"Some things can't happen unless you talk about them first."

"I'll have to think about that," Robbie said, smiling at his friend.

"I may take Coach Preston up on trying my hand in right field. Give Diskin some competition, which couldn't hurt him. Besides, I'd have plenty of time to think out there. Seems made to order for a philosophy major."

"You serious?" asked Robbie.

"Philosophy majors are *always* serious," said Wally. Then he winked. "Except when we're not."

"It's just one game, Wally," said Robbie. "Nothing's set yet."

"Maybe. But you showed a lot of heart out there today. And you came through in the clutch. More important, you brought the whole team together. Freshman or not, you're the one the guys are going to look to now to lead the way."

"Me?" Robbie said in genuine surprise. "Nah, I don't think—"

"That's right, Robbie," Wally said, cutting him off. "Don't think right now. Enjoy. You just caught a perfect game!"

In the locker room, it seemed everyone on the team stopped by Robbie's locker to congratulate him on his play. Hank Greengrass brought his father into the locker room. Gus Greengrass shook Robbie's hand and said, "You look like Show material to me, kid! Unlike some people I know." Then Gus gave his son a disappointed look. Hank had gone hitless in the season opener.

Robbie was thrilled to meet one of his childhood heroes. But he wondered why Gus Greengrass would make his son feel worse than he already did. "If anybody's Show material," said Robbie, "it's Hank. A chip off the old block!"

Gus Greengrass laughed nervously and slapped Robbie's back. "We'll see," he said. "We'll see."

When Eagle finally came in after all his interviews, he acted a little upset at the people thanking Robbie!

"I'm the one that threw the perfect game, not him!" he said at one point. Robbie saw other players roll their eyes at this.

"Well, Eagle, you pitched great," said Robbie. "A no-hitter is tough enough. But a perfect game, well, you can't even make one mistake! It was awesome. My hat goes off to you!" And with that, Robbie took off his cap, and everyone else on the team did, too. They cheered their pitcher and waved their red and brown hats in homage.

Robbie and Cynthia went out to eat with Robbie's parents after the game. His parents also invited Brian Webster and Joshua Kenny, who gladly accepted. The talk during dinner centered on Eagle and his perfect game. Cynthia was hoping that the extra fame this gave Eagle would keep him from bothering her anymore. Robbie hoped so, too. But he didn't think it would be that easy.

Joshua talked about how much he missed his girlfriend, Melinda Clark, who was away at Whalen University. Everybody at the table knew Melinda well. Robbie had grown up with Melinda. She lived a couple of houses down from him. Melinda had gone to Riverton High School and had been a big help to the baseball team. She kept statistics, took videos, and scouted for them.

Melinda and Joshua had been dating each other for about four years. Last year, Josh had gone out a few times with Cynthia's roommate, Dori. This had led to some tension between Josh and Melinda, so he had stopped dating Dori.

Brian had developed a crush on Melinda last year, something he never told Joshua about. When Brian had finally summoned up enough courage to tell Melinda, she had been understanding but honest. She told Brian she was interested in him only as a friend. Brian took it well. At least, that's the way it seemed.

Robbie felt sorry for Brian. Robbie knew what it was like to get shut out romantically. In the past, he and Cynthia had periods when there was little or no contact between them. Those times hurt, and Robbie wondered if somehow Brian was still hurting—inside.

After the dinner, Robbie's parents began their three-hour drive home. Robbie and his friends went to Redstone's student union building to hang out. Around ten o'clock, Eagle showed up, flushed with celebration for his perfect game.

Everyone in the student union stood up and gave Eagle an ovation! Eagle beamed and bowed grandly. The cheers eventually faded, and the students went back to what they were doing before his entrance. Eagle looked a little disappointed that the cheers had ended so soon. He and Wally Potenza, who trailed behind him, walked toward the table where Robbie and his friends were sitting.

"Hi, Cynthia!" the pitcher said, a smug smile on his face. "I suppose you might be willing to talk with me now."

"Congratulations on your perfect game, Eagle," she said evenly.

" 'Congratulations on your perfect game, Eagle,' " Eagle mimicked. "Is that all you can say?"

"Come on, Eagle," Wally said, taking his friend's arm. "We'd better get going."

"Forget it, Wally!" Eagle said, yanking his arm away. "What about it, Cynthia? Is that all you're going to say?"

"I do have something else to say," Cynthia said softly.

"You're going to ask me to join you?" Eagle asked.

"No, I'm not, Eagle, because you're making me feel uncomfortable. But I do want to say one thing. It wasn't *your* perfect game only. It was your whole team's."

"Is that what Belmont's been telling you?" said Eagle, a wild look in his eye.

"It's what everyone in the stands was saying. Robbie keeps calling it your perfect game."

"You're lying," said Eagle. "You never were very good at being honest, Cynthia."

"That's enough, Eagle," said Robbie.

"It is NOT enough!" Eagle screamed, slamming his hand on their table. The dishes and glasses rattled and clinked. The student union grew suddenly quiet.

Eagle's face was two inches from Robbie's. After a tense pause, Robbie smiled and said, "Don't forget the press, Eagle. Over there."

Eagle's eyes flicked to the tables shared by the students who worked for the campus newspaper. "Just smile back at me, friend," Robbie went on in a whisper, "and we'll pretend we were just joking."

Robbie could almost see the wheels turning in Eagle's head. Eagle didn't want bad publicity to taint his pitching feat.

Eagle forced a smile on his face. Then he said through gritted teeth, "This isn't over yet, Belmont." With that, Eagle gave Robbie a clap on the back. The pitcher walked over happily to the student reporters and greeted them. Wally stayed

65

behind to apologize to Cynthia and Robbie. He ended up staying at their table.

The evening went on without further hassle from Eagle. But there was one more disturbing thing that happened. At one point, Robbie noticed that Joshua was no longer around. He asked Brian where Joshua had gone, and an odd look came over Brian's face. "Josh left with Dori."

"Uh-oh," said Robbie.

"Dori told me she wouldn't go out with Josh unless he broke up with Melinda," said Cynthia.

"Love may make the world go 'round," said Wally, "but sometimes it also seems to make the world fall apart."

"Still, what else can we do?" asked Robbie.

Eagle was glaring over at their table again. Robbie sighed. He knew one thing Eagle had said was true. It wasn't over yet.

Chapter Six

The college baseball season was a lot more demanding than the high-school season. Riverton High School had only averaged about twenty-five games a season. Redstone University had sixty! Frank Preston tried to schedule it so that Eagle pitched to the good teams and Clem Goodall pitched to the not-so-good.

The arrangement worked surprisingly well. The Colts were winning most of their games, though they were not winning them in a commanding way. They were scratching out late-inning rallies to overtake their opponents. A strange combination of grit and luck made the Colts keep coming out on top. "The Colts look bad, but win good," one national magazine said.

Robbie's teacher for Descriptive Writing discussed the article in class. He said it should be "The Colts look bad, but win *well*."

Robbie was doing better in this course, but still not as well as he wanted. The B he got on his essay about the bat was the highest grade he'd received so far. In fact, Robbie was getting B's or C's in all his courses except Speech. In Speech, he was getting an A!

Robbie's Speech class helped build up his confidence in speaking with his teammates. He especially liked to make the guys laugh. Robbie wasn't the team comic—there were a number of other guys who were much funnier. But what few laughs Robbie provided seemed to lift the sagging spirits of the Colts. That made *him* feel good, too.

Team morale was suffering. Eagle's dark moods and bad temper made it hard to get a long happy streak going. If good feelings started to grow, before long Eagle would storm by or throw a piece of equipment around. His mood sometimes passed on to others, and they'd throw equipment around, too.

Nothing ever feels good on this team for very long! Robbie thought. It bothered him. It also bothered Oscar Gonzales. He was the team captain and shortstop. Oscar got along well with Robbie. At times, the two would talk about the team's morale problem.

What complicated the problem was that Eagle Wilson was pitching better than ever. If Eagle had been throwing badly, his teammates would not hesitate to tell him to stop being such a drag. But after two weeks, Eagle had five wins and no losses. His head swelled with each victory. And if anyone criticized him, he blew up.

Even Wally, Eagle's closest friend on the team, was losing patience with him. "You know what Eagle's best pitch is?" Wally once asked Robbie.

"A curve ball?"

"Nope. A tantrum. Eagle throws that better than anything else."

Frank Preston had several talks with Eagle. But when the coach wasn't around, Eagle would still explode. Baseball was supposed to be fun— and Eagle was making it anything but. It was exhausting to play a full game and then to defuse Eagle's bombs.

Robbie was afraid Eagle's antics were hurting Robbie's own game. His catching was strong— not one error or passed ball had been scored against him yet. But Robbie's hitting was still disappointing. His average was .250, the lowest of his life. One hit every four at-bats wasn't what Robbie was used to. He knew batting averages in college were usually lower than in high school. But college batting averages were still higher than pro ball averages. Major-college batting champions usually hit over .440—and some hit over .500!

Robbie knew .250 was not the average of a good hitter. It was the average of a good catcher who couldn't hit well. No matter how much the major leagues needed catchers, pro scouts would still take little notice of one who hit so poorly in college. Robbie began to worry that his best baseball days were over.

But still the Redstone Colts kept winning ball games! And Robbie kept knocking runs in. Low as his batting average was, he was leading the team in runs batted in. His batting average with men in scoring position was .425! Something about the whole team needing him gave Robbie the extra concentration to hit in the clutch. It was an unusual talent that Robbie didn't mind having.

It was usually a lot more fun playing in the games Eagle didn't start. Coach Preston made Eagle stay in the bullpen those days. That way, Eagle's grouchiness didn't bother most of the team.

Robbie really enjoyed catching on the days when Clem Goodall pitched. Clem was a light-haired, freckled, big sophomore who grew up on a farm with ten brothers and sisters. It seemed there was nothing that could rattle Clem. He had a dry sense of humor, and he wasn't afraid to use it on himself.

Clem could throw the ball eighty-five miles an hour, and his control wasn't bad. But his fast ball didn't hop much. It moved a little on some pitches, but not enough to count on.

Robbie understood Clem's fast-ball problem. All during grammar school, Robbie was a star pitcher. But when he got to Riverton High School, Coach Gus Franklin thought catcher suited Robbie best. Robbie remembered how stunned he was at the coach's decision. Lack of movement on his fast ball was one of the main reasons the coach gave for his decision.

Robbie had finally gotten over his desire to be a pitcher. He had grown to love catching as much as he loved to hit. And being a catcher was one of the quickest ways to the majors. But every once in a while, Robbie passed the mound and stopped to stand on the pitching rubber. It was a grand view with pitcher's eyes. No iron bars masked your sight! But Robbie's fast ball went too straight. Just like Clem's.

Robbie worked with Clem on developing a hop. He showed Clem how to throw a cutter fast ball. Clem learned how to put extra pressure on the ball with his middle finger to make the fast ball bend in to a right-handed hitter. Clem got used to throwing it more sidearm as well. By the middle of the season, Clem's fast ball had developed a small but nasty in-shoot.

Robbie also worked on Clem's split-fingered fast ball. Everyone called it a "splitter." It had a sharp, last-second drop and the speed of a good fast ball. If Clem could develop his splitter, he could be as winning a pitcher as Eagle.

71

The Colts' relief work was handled mostly by the Conklin twins, Roger and Wyatt. The twins were quite a pair. They had a weird way of talking with one another sometimes that only they could understand.

"Snake eyes!" Roger called out once when Robbie leaned across him.

From the other end of the bullpen came Wyatt's response. "Those snake eyes are closed!"

"Why did you say 'snake eyes'?" Robbie asked Roger. Roger had a milder personality than Wyatt.

"No one asks that," Roger said, a look of surprise on his face.

"Except me," Robbie said with a smile.

"I said 'snake eyes' because you leaned across me like a snake all of a sudden."

"That's something like what I thought," said Robbie. "So when Wyatt said the snake eyes were closed, did that mean 'Don't worry, he's no threat'?"

"Yeah, I guess," said Roger, looking hard at Robbie. Wyatt joined them. "He understands," Roger told his twin.

"Yeah?" said Wyatt, chewing a big wad of gum. "That's good."

"Good for a catcher," said Robbie. "But let me ask you something. Why don't you just say it right out, without the code?"

"It's part of the fun."

"Yeah. Codes come in handy, too."

They were a weird duo, but Robbie began to get along with them. He was one of the first players on the team to carry on a conversation longer than three sentences with them. Robbie often wondered what it was like in the bullpen when Eagle was with the "Conks."

Their relief pitching was weak in the first part of the season. But as Robbie got to know them and their pitching strengths, the Conklin twins began to get hot. Roger threw the ball real hard and had a little but effective sinker. He was used for short relief and often came in with men on base. Wyatt was Mr. Junk Man—knucklers, fork balls, palm balls, screwballs, off-speed drops, and a fast ball that wasn't bad. He was used more for long relief.

Wally Potenza was eventually successful in his bid for right field. He told Frank Preston he was interested in the position. Frank tried him there and liked what he saw. At first, Coach Preston platooned Wally with Charlie Diskin. By the twentieth game of the season, Wally had a better batting average and more runs batted in than Charlie. So Wally became the Colts' starting right fielder when the Colts' record was eighteen wins and two losses. Wally was batting a crisp .302.

Despite Robbie's low .250 batting average, there was no longer any doubt he was the starting catcher. Even Eagle preferred Robbie to Wally now. Eagle was still trying to get another perfect game each time he pitched. He was determined to be the first college pitcher ever to get two of them. Robbie encouraged Eagle in this goal.

Eagle had many games where he'd pitch perfect baseball for three or four innings. Then a walk or an error would end his chances. "Go for a no-hitter!" Robbie would call to Eagle at that point. And Eagle would! But then his no-hitter would be broken. "Go for a shutout!" Robbie would call. And Eagle would. But whenever the shutout was broken, Eagle would get all huffy. At that point, it was very hard to get Eagle to give his all.

But in the twenty-fifth game of the season, Robbie finally hit on something to keep Eagle psyched up. After an opponent had broken Eagle's no-hitter in the fifth inning with a bloop single, Robbie went out to Eagle on the mound. The Colts were ahead, 4–0. Eagle was kicking the dirt around the mound and muttering.

"You'll never get another perfect game, Eagle," Robbie said.

"What?" Eagle asked in shock.

"You know why you'll never get another perfect game or even a no-hitter? Because you don't practice enough!"

"You can't practice for that and you know it, Belmont," said Eagle defensively. "You either do it or don't."

"What do you mean you can't practice it? You *can* practice it. Want to throw a perfect game? Then make every pitch a perfect game pitch. If you can't, practice. *Hard*. That's the quickest way to make it happen, Eags."

Eagle was quiet for a while. Then he said something that nearly made Robbie faint. "You're right."

Since that mound chat, Eagle Wilson started throwing every pitch as if his life depended on it. By the thirtieth game, his earned run average was 1.85, and his win-loss record was 12–3! And with every complete game he pitched, the number of batters he faced got closer to that "perfect" twenty-seven.

The Redstone Colts kept winning but still didn't feel like a team. Robbie kept thinking about it, wondering what he could do. The team never hung out together very much. There were few new friendships formed since the season began. Players usually hung out in the same small groups of twos or threes.

Robbie, though a freshman, seemed to be making friends with more players than most. He already knew Brian and Joshua from high school, and they were always hanging around. Robbie was also getting to be friends with Wally Potenza and the team captain, Oscar Gonzales.

Redstone's center fielder, Hank Greengrass, was another teammate Robbie was getting to know better. After the season opener, Hank went on a tear, hitting .340. His father, Gus, came to most of Redstone's home games and a few away games. During a bus ride to an away game where Gus Greengrass would not be present, Hank and Robbie sat together. That's when Hank first opened up about his famous father.

"You know, Robbie, he always says I can do better, that I *should* be doing better. No matter how many hits I get or how many fly balls I run down, Dad's always telling me to do better." Hank looked out the bus window, then turned back to Robbie. "It's getting to the point where I hope he *isn't* in the stands when I play."

"I think he means well," said Robbie, trying to be of some help.

"Yeah, I know he does. But that's not the point. I feel he's standing beside me all the time—with a frown on his face. Know what I mean?"

"Expectations," said Robbie with a long, drawn-out sigh. "No easy load to carry, whether they're your own or someone else's."

"Exactly," said Hank. "And the pressure just builds and builds."

"I'll tell you something, Hank," said Robbie in all seriousness, "I'm worried I might never hit above .300 again."

"You will. No sweat. Just keep swinging

away. The hits will fall for you sooner or later."

"Ha! Easy for you to say!"

"I suppose," said Hank, looking back out the window. "But you will anyway. Believe it."

Chapter Seven

Team morale started to improve. The Redstone Colts began winning games with a little more authority. Robbie felt good about that. But he felt terrible about his hitting. Even though his RBI total was still fairly good, his batting average dropped from .250 to .194. He was in a miserable slump.

The day after his average dropped below .200, Robbie took serious stock of himself. He talked with Coach Preston about it. They were on the team bus, riding to an away game. Frank Preston looked mildly surprised when Robbie asked him how to get out of his slump.

"You're in a slump, you call it?" the manager asked at first. Then he thought a bit and said, "Yeah, I guess you are. Lately, you haven't even been bringing the runs home as well, that's true.

78

But you've been hitting the ball hard—just right at the fielders."

It was true—Robbie had been hitting the ball right at fielders. This could be considered bad luck rather than bad hitting. But after doing it so often, Robbie wondered if his body was missing the little clues that helped him "hit 'em where they ain't." And lately, he had been failing to hit even with men on base. This was the most disturbing part of his performance so far.

"Eddie Trent said something about slumps the other day in the paper," said Coach Preston.

Eddie Trent was Robbie's favorite major-league player, a six-time all-star catcher for the New York Titans. Robbie had met Eddie Trent several times. Eddie was a close friend of Robbie's high-school coach, Gus Franklin, and had coached Robbie's side of a national high-school all-star game last summer.

Eddie Trent was also having a slump this year, the first long one for him Robbie could remember. Eddie's average, usually over .300, was only .241. The reporters were starting to ask him about his "slump." As usual, Eddie was honest in his replies.

"What Eddie Trent said," Frank Preston continued, "was that in a slump the most important thing to remember is to 'keep the windshield wipers going.' "

Robbie laughed. It made sense. A slump was

like nonstop rain. It seemed to dampen everything. It could also blur your vision and even drown you if you let it.

"I guess keeping the wipers going means keeping your eye on the ball, keeping things as clear as possible until the rain stops." Robbie was talking more to himself than to Coach Preston. "It means I should keep trying, not lose faith in myself, even though nothing seems to be working."

"Couldn't have said it better myself, Robbie," said the coach, smiling.

There was a moment of silence as the two watched the scenery roll past the window of the bus. The wind had kicked up, bending the treetops and tall grass along the roadway. It was also getting dark, though it was still early in the afternoon.

"You know, Robbie, there's something about a slump that just plain can't be figured out," offered the coach. "Maybe the best thing to do is just accept that you'll have slumps every once in a while. But don't let them get you too crazy. Maybe that's the best thing."

"Should I try changing my swing at all?" Robbie asked.

"To my eye, your swing is still smooth. Sometimes you step too soon out of eagerness, but not that often. Your back elbow is up. Your swing is level. Your hips rotate well through the swing. Maybe something is affecting your concentration. The first year of college can be tough on anyone. Lot of adjustments."

"I'll tell you one thing, Coach, I wish the team were a closer unit. That weighs heavier on my mind than anything else, I think."

It was true. Robbie hadn't realized it until he said it, but there it was. *I care about this team! I worry—too much, maybe—about how everyone gets along.*

"That's what makes you a good catcher, Robbie," said Frank Preston. "I think you're right. This team hasn't really jelled yet. I've managed at Redstone for ten years now, and this is the strangest bunch yet. I've never had a team with more talent, and I've never had a team that got along this badly! How do you figure that?"

Before Robbie could reply, the sky opened up outside. A flash of lightning and a crack of thunder were followed by a heavy rain. Robbie rubbed the side window of the bus with his palm. He still couldn't see out of it.

But looking forward, he could see the road ahead of the bus. The driver was whistling as the wipers slapped back and forth on the windshield.

Just keep the wipers going, Robbie thought to himself.

Chapter Eight

There was a lot of traveling involved in college baseball. Robbie traveled by plane, train, bus, and car when the team went on the road. Playing thirty away games meant he was away from campus and Cynthia a lot of the baseball season. *This might be a taste of what it would be like to be a married pro ball player on a road trip*, thought Robbie.

The traveling made for good adventure. Seeing a new place and doing new things were fun. But it was also hard living out of duffel bags and not having a home base. At times, it could be very lonely. At times, it could make a batting slump feel like a life slump.

There were other times, however, that were great. This road trip for the Colts' fortieth game was one of them. They were playing Whalen University, the school Melinda Clark attended.

Joshua, Brian, and Robbie were all looking forward in different ways to seeing Melinda again. Brian wanted to see her because he still had strong feelings toward her. Robbie wanted to see Melinda because he wanted her to videotape his batting and help get him out of his slump. But Josh wanted to see her most of all. There had been tension lately between them because he had dated Dori, Cynthia Wu's roommate. Josh and Melinda needed to talk face to face.

Redstone's record at this time was thirty wins and nine losses. The Colts had a very good chance at making the post-season tournament that led to the College World Series. The Whalen University Pilgrims didn't have much of a baseball team. But everyone who played on it did so because he loved the game. Their record was six wins and thirty-three losses. The annual Redstone-Whalen game was usually an enjoyable one, which the Colts had never lost.

Melinda's videotape gear was ready when Robbie came up to bat. Redstone University also videotaped their baseball games. But Melinda's tapes would concentrate on Robbie's batting with more close-ups. Melinda had also brought along some videotapes of Robbie batting in high school for comparison. Melinda's observations had helped Robbie out of slumps in high school. Now, maybe she could help him out of this monster college slump.

To put Robbie's high RBI power to better use, Frank Preston had moved Robbie up a notch in the batting order. Robbie now hit fifth instead of sixth, switching spots with Lou Ranger. The Redstone manager's confidence in Robbie encouraged him a lot.

Robbie first came up with two outs and two men on. Oscar Gonzales was on second, and Wally Potenza was on first. The Pilgrims' pitcher was Terry Lioni. He was a friend of Melinda Clark's. They shared an interest in computers.

Terry wasn't the greatest pitcher, but he gave his all. He tried to sneak a fast ball past Robbie, and Robbie hauled off on it. His homer easily cleared the left-field fence. He drove in three runs with one strong stroke.

Robbie had known he was going to get a hit. He usually felt that way with men on base. Not that he got a hit *every* time he was up in that situation. It was just that he felt different with men on base. He wasn't worried about batting then. His slump, in fact, was only when he was batting with no one on base. In thirty-nine games so far, he had eight homers with men on base but only two with no one on. *I should have at least six solo homers*, Robbie thought as he trotted around the bases with his head down.

Robbie enjoyed the pats and high fives he got after he crossed home. He sat down on the bench and remembered that Melinda had videotaped that blast. *Oh, well,* he thought. *Maybe it won't help my slump, but it'll be nice to see a close-up of me hitting well for a change!*

Clem Goodall started for the Colts. He took the mound in the bottom of the first. The Colts' 3–0 lead gave Clem the confidence to hurl without worry. His fast ball's hop was a little livelier than usual. His newly developed cutter fast ball drew weak handle-hit grounders from the first two Pilgrim batters. The third batter, Whalen's best hitter, swung over three straight sinking splitters. Clem was looking fresh and smart today. He was throwing with a loose, hitch-free motion.

Robbie batted in the third inning with no one on base. Terry Lioni threw Robbie a little curve that almost made Robbie drool with anticipation. But Robbie's rippling swing undercut the ball, sending a long, high fly to the center fielder. The wind got hold of it, but it didn't matter. Whalen's center fielder lunged and made a great catch of the ball on the warning path.

There was one out in the fifth inning when Robbie came to the plate for the third time. Hank Greengrass was in scoring position on second base. But Robbie hit a line drive right into the third baseman's glove. Whalen's third baseman threw the ball right away to second, doubling Hank off the bag for the third and final out of Redstone's inning.

The score was 7–0 in favor of the Colts by the seventh inning. Robbie came up to the plate for his fourth at-bat. There was no one on and two outs. Terry Lioni's arm was very tired by now, and his fast ball had lost almost all its steam. Robbie took a crack at the first pitch, a gopher ball down the middle. He didn't try to kill the ball, but he took extra care to make sure he connected cleanly.

He did connect cleanly—but with no power! The ball bounced routinely to the shortstop. Robbie was thrown out by three yards. He ran back to the dugout shaking his head. He wanted to see Melinda's video of that poor excuse of a hit. *How can I hit such a miserable grounder after hitting such a homer earlier?* he wondered. As far as Robbie was concerned, that was the biggest mystery in baseball!

One of the best surprises of this contest was that Clem was pitching a perfect game, matching Eagle's performance in the opener. This not only improved Coach Preston's opinion of Clem's pitching, but also of Robbie's catching. Robbie was the common factor in the two perfect game performances. His handling of pitchers and knowledge of batters were impressive in a major-league way.

Unknown to Robbie, the New York Titans' scout Mack Doogan had asked Frank Preston a few times about Robbie. Preston's report was careful but favorable. He spoke well of Robbie's catching, speed, and RBI production. He also praised Robbie's growing leadership among the Colt players.

Clem Goodall's perfect game ended in the seventh inning. It was as if his arm suddenly said, "Enough! I'm not perfect!" First, Clem hit a Whalen batter, then walked the next one. The third batter in the inning got the Pilgrims' first hit of the day. It was a sharp single up the middle that brought one run home. The fourth batter then whomped a hanging curve ball and cleared the bases with a three-run homer. In three minutes, the game had gone from Clem's perfect game with a 7–0 lead to a 7–4 contest!

Frank Preston took Clem out and brought in the Colts' short-relief pitcher, Roger Conklin. After Roger threw his warm-ups, Robbie went out to the mound to discuss signals with him. After getting them straight, Roger got an amused look in his eyes and said to Robbie, "I think ol' Eagle's going a little batty out there in the bullpen today."

"How?" asked Robbie, concerned.

"He's been mumbling Cynthia Wu's name over and over again," said Roger with his goofy grin.

"Oh, no," said Robbie. He thought Eagle had been getting better lately.

"Eagle thinks we twins are so weird that we'd hardly notice something like that, I guess," said

Roger. "He shuts his eyes and chants, 'Cynthia Wu, Cynthia Woooo!' And he thinks *we're* weird! He's driving Wyatt and me nutso out there. It's a relief to be here on the mound!"

"It's *always* a relief when you're on the mound." Here, Robbie smiled. "After all, you're a relief pitcher."

Roger just looked at Robbie. "I hate puns."

"Hey, just trying to lighten things up a bit," said Robbie, still smiling. Then he turned serious. "Whalen's bats are coming alive. Feel like putting them back to sleep?"

Roger smiled in his lazy way. "Give me two minutes and this inning is history!" he said.

Roger was as good as his word. In a quick, no-nonsense way, he closed out the inning.

Robbie came to bat one last time in the top of the ninth inning. The Pilgrims' second relief pitcher tried throwing Robbie a change-up curve. Robbie wasn't fooled by it. He waited patiently for the floating spinner and ripped it to left field. The left fielder took two steps to his right and snagged the line drive like a frog snapping a buzzing fly. Robbie was one for five at the plate today, a .200 batting performance.

He sure was getting sick of having his hard-hit balls swallowed on the fly by opponents! He was tempted to throw equipment himself, but he resisted the idea. Robbie felt sour, but he didn't want the team's spirit to suffer.

Roger Conklin finished the game allowing no walks or hits. The Colts won, 7–4. The pitchers, with Robbie's help, had allowed just two hits! Robbie dressed quietly and tried to keep a cheerful face. But he felt sick to his stomach.

After showering and dressing, he confronted Eagle about his weird behavior. Eagle flatly denied it. But then the Conklin twins walked by, muttering "Woooo, Woooo" like a locomotive whistle.

"Very funny, you goons!" Eagle shouted after them.

The Conklins' laughter could be heard even after they had left the locker room. Robbie tried to tell Eagle that chanting Cynthia's name would not win her back, and it also wouldn't be good if the rest of the team and the coaches found out about it.

Eagle said nothing in reply. He left in a huff.

It was very busy in Melinda's dormitory room that night! Terry Lioni brought over his videocassette recorder and hooked it up to Melinda's TV. Robbie spent most of the visit watching Melinda's videotape of his batting. Melinda was only able to watch a little bit of it, as she had other visitors: mainly Joshua, but also Brian and even Terry Lioni! Terry said he had heard so much about Joshua from Melinda that he wanted to meet him for himself. Robbie got the impression Terry was more interested in being with Melinda than in meeting Joshua.

Terry watched some of the videotape with Robbie. He winced when Robbie hit the homer off his gopher ball. But Terry had no hard feelings about it. He knew as much as he loved the game, baseball was not in his future after college.

Robbie couldn't see anything wrong with his hitting style from the videotape. Then Melinda came over again for another look. She popped out the tape and put in one of Robbie hitting in high school.

"There!" she said, freezing the action on the screen and pointing to it. "That's what you *should* be doing."

Robbie understood. He was regularly making contact with the ball a few inches in front of where he had usually made contact in high school. This little detail showed a great deal.

In simple terms, Robbie was stepping and swinging too soon. Two tenths of a second may seem like a small amount of time. But to a batter, it represented the difference between lunging at the ball and hitting it with control! The split second would give Robbie's keen eyes an important extra glimpse at the ball. It could give his body the time it needed to sense where to drive the ball. It could mean the difference between hitting the ball where the fielders stood or hitting it in the gaps.

Terry seemed as excited by the discovery as Robbie. He pointed out that Robbie had hit his home-run ball closer to the plate than all his other hits. When men were on base, Robbie waited that extra moment to make sure he got the best look possible at the pitch. His responsibility to the team made him give it that additional, split-second look. If he could only do that now with every pitch, Robbie might start hitting as he should again.

At Terry's urging, Robbie watched his home run over and over. Terry pointed out how relaxed and simple Robbie looked as he hit it. Robbie remembered the feeling at the moment of contact. *That easy, simple feeling—I'll have to work on remembering that*, Robbie resolved.

Robbie was happy with the discovery and eager to try it out in the batter's box. He thanked Melinda profusely and gave her a brotherly kiss on the cheek. Brian said good night to her, too, but didn't give her a kiss because he felt anything but brotherly toward her! Terry stayed to play with Melinda's computer while she talked with Joshua Kenny. Joshua didn't look too happy. Robbie got the impression that Josh and Melinda had worked things out about Josh dating Dori. But Terry Lioni hanging around made Josh realize there were other people interested in dating Melinda.

On the way back to the hotel where the team

was staying, Brian told Robbie how much he still liked Melinda. "And she knows it," said Robbie's long-time friend. "She tried to be nice to me, but somehow that makes me feel worse. I think it would be better if I didn't write her anymore. But then I wouldn't get any more letters from her."

Robbie said nothing. He never knew how to advise Brian about Melinda. But just listening seemed to help a little.

Later that night, Robbie called Cynthia and told her of the day's events. He was still excited about having found what might be the cause of his slump. "Overeagerness!" he told her. "I should've known that by now!"

They talked about Melinda, Joshua, Brian, Terry Lioni, and Dori. Cynthia said Dori had vowed not to date Josh again. Robbie and Cynthia then talked about how confusing human relationships were. They were glad that theirs seemed clear and strong. It was a rare, special thing in his life, Robbie told her. He never meant anything more.

After hanging up, Robbie sat without moving for about ten minutes. He had a great woman in his life. He should be a happy young man.

He just had to stop stepping and swinging too soon!

Chapter Nine

So Robbie started working on waiting a bit longer before he swung. He spent extra time batting against the pitching machine. He was working very hard on swinging patiently. It was not easy. But Robbie got to the point where he felt a little more control swinging. Still, he was far from satisfied.

In the next game, Robbie did his best not to step too soon. But he had no hits in four at-bats. The Redstone Colts lost the game, 2–1. It was their tenth defeat of the season.

Robbie watched the videotape of the game with the whole team the next Monday. The tape didn't show Robbie as closely as Melinda's, but it was close enough. He was *still* swinging too soon, despite his determination not to. It was such a hard habit to break!

Robbie continued to work on waiting for the

ball. Brian Webster borrowed a video camera and made tapes of Robbie's batting practices. But in the next game, Robbie again went zero for four at the plate! There were men on base three of the four times he was up—and he failed to bring any of them home! His slump was spreading like a disease through all his batting now. Robbie's only comfort was that the Colts won the game, 5–2. Everyone else hit but Robbie.

Robbie didn't know what to do. He grew very worried. The more he worried, the tighter his swing became. The longer his slump went on, the more pressure he felt to break it. The more pressure he felt to break it, the harder it was to swing easily. He only had one hit in Redstone's next game. But it was a satisfying hit, a game-winning home run in the ninth inning.

Meanwhile, as a catcher, he had the constant satisfaction of seeing the team grow closer. In the next game, for example, there was a play that showed how the teamwork was getting better. There was a very high pop-up over the first-base line. Robbie, Eagle, first baseman Jeff Streets, and second baseman Sidney Fisher all converged on the ball. Robbie was talking from the start.

"I can get this, I can get this," he said as soon as Jeff Streets was in earshot.

They both stood about a yard apart, saying

94

nothing as the ball started to descend. Then Jeff said, "I got this."

"It's yours. Jeff's!" Robbie said, getting down on one knee, ready to grab the ball if it came out of Jeff's glove. Sidney and Eagle stood by. Then Sidney went down on one knee on the other side of Jeff, who was now zeroing in on the ball.

Suddenly, Eagle shouted, "I have this! Look out!"

Robbie didn't hesitate. "Back off," he said quietly but firmly. "It's Jeff's."

Eagle grumbled but went down on his knee, too. Jeff Streets caught the pop-up, then looked at the three kneeling players surrounding him. "I wish you guys would show me this much respect off the field, too!" Jeff said, smiling.

The Colts prided themselves on how the fielders talked among themselves. Robbie had a lot to do with that team trait.

There were some great individual performances that kept Redstone winning. In their forty-fifth game, the Colts were ahead by one run in the bottom of the ninth. With two outs, a runner tried to steal second in order to get into scoring position. Wyatt Conklin was pitching. His slow, dipping knuckler gave the runner a big jump, so Robbie had to hurry his throw. Since the batter was left-handed, the shortstop was covering the bag. Robbie's peg steamed but went wide on the first-base side of second. Oscar Gonzales leapt for the wild throw. He caught it barehanded and tagged the sliding runner in the same motion!

Eagle's moods were still a problem. But the team got more and more used to them and learned to deal with them. They developed a united front against his dramatics. In a strange way, Eagle's weirdness was bringing the team closer. But it wasn't a total closeness. The team would get much closer if Eagle *stopped* acting strange. Robbie and Wally Potenza often talked about ways of getting Eagle sane again.

"There's a whole side of him only a few people ever see," Wally said one night. Wally and Robbie were walking to the dining hall after practice.

"I guess you and Cynthia are two of those few people," Robbie said.

"Maybe. But he doesn't show it at all to Cynthia anymore. I see this good side from time to time. When we go to a movie, say, or goof off on a study break, he's fun, easy to be with. But the minute Cynthia comes into the picture, he goes into his act, whining and being a pain to everyone."

At this moment, they heard a voice calling behind them. "Hey, Wally! Wait up!"

It was Eagle Wilson. He trotted up to them. "Hi, Wally." Eagle paused, then spoke again. "Hi, Belmont." Eagle looked back at Wally. "Hey, want to catch some grub with me at the dining hall? Tonight's special: mystery meat!"

"Why should tonight's special be different from

any other night's," said Wally. "Robbie and I were just heading over."

"Oh," said Eagle. He didn't know what to say.

"Want to join us?" asked Wally.

"Well . . ."

"Come on, Eags," prodded Wally. "You can carry this thing only so far, you know."

"All right, then," Eagle finally said, "let's go."

On the way over to the dining hall, the three Colt ball players exchanged hellos with a number of other students. At one point, Eagle suddenly ran away ten yards and snagged a Frisbee that had been thrown wildly. He then whirled and threw it back about fifty yards. It was a perfect chest-high sail. Robbie, Wally, and the students who had seen the maneuver clapped. Eagle made a couple of mock bows, grinning broadly.

Surprisingly, the three had a good time at dinner. Wally and Eagle kept up a constant banter that Robbie enjoyed. Robbie didn't say much, but that seemed okay with them. By dessert, they were discussing philosophy. Robbie was surprised to learn this was something Eagle loved to do. Eagle seemed to be in a good mood this evening. His eyes were bright as he listened to what Wally was saying.

Robbie left them after an hour. He had an assignment on Shakespeare to prepare for tomorrow's Speech class. Wally and Eagle stayed and continued talking.

A few days later, the Redstone Colts took a train to their fiftieth game. Their record now was 35–14. Robbie and Wally sat together for most of the long trip.

"Eagle and I talked for about three more hours after you left," Wally told Robbie.

"Do you think he'll be able to get back into the swing of things with the team?"

"Actually, I do. He admitted that he didn't miss Cynthia as much as he pretended to. 'I just like being dramatic sometimes,' he said. Toward the end, he even admitted he may have been acting 'a little like a jerk,' as he described it. Progress is being made."

Eagle's improved mood started showing up that very game. He threw a no-hitter. It would have been a perfect game, but with one out Sidney Fisher bobbled a routine grounder in the fourth inning for an error. Eagle started to yell at Sidney. Robbie called out, "Come on, Eagle, help him out."

Eagle stopped, then said, "It's all right, Sid! Don't worry about it!"

Still, Eagle walked the next two batters. Robbie could see him struggling to keep his temper. The following batter hit a high bouncing ball. Sid leapt up to get the ball, then slung it to second as he was coming down. Oscar threw the relay to first, nipping the runner for a double play. The rally was stopped and the inning was over.

Eagle cheered and ran over to give a high five to Sidney.

Eagle is definitely improving, Robbie thought. *Maybe this team has a chance to go far after all!* Robbie felt a great relief flooding through him. If Eagle could become a help rather than a hindrance, Robbie's work would become a lot easier.

At the plate, Robbie got two singles in four at-bats. It was the first time he had hit .500 in a game all year. The singles had not felt confident, but they were singles all the same.

The next five games were all scheduled at Redstone Stadium. Being around Cynthia more raised Robbie's spirits a lot. And one day during batting practice, Hank Greengrass helped Robbie find that easy, simple feeling at the plate again.

Jay Manning was pitching batting practice and throwing fairly hard to Robbie. Assistant Coach Manning threw a pitch that slipped, and it went way high. Robbie didn't swing at it for a hit. He swung just to knock it back to Jay. He swung softly, tapping it neatly back to Jay on two hops. The next pitch was also bad, high and inside. Robbie nimbly backed away and again knocked the bad pitch neatly back to Jay.

"That's it, Robbie!" Hank Greengrass called excitedly from the bench.

"What's it?" asked Robbie.

"Your timing when you tapped those bad pitches back to the mound!" said Hank. "Those were hard pitches to hit, and yet you hit them with perfect control."

"Yeah, but only back to the pitcher," said Robbie with a shrug.

"But somehow, when you decided you weren't going to swing full blast at the ball, the pressure dropped off. Then your timing was perfect! So maybe try this: Right before you swing, tell yourself it's a bad pitch. Then just tap it over the left-field fence!"

Robbie laughed. He thought he knew what Hank meant. Right before swinging, he would tell himself the pressure was off.

Jay Manning now threw a fat gopher ball down the middle. Robbie pretended it was a pitch he normally would let go. At the last split second before his swing, he said to himself, *Just tap it over the fence.*

And that's exactly what he did.

The crack of the bat turned all his teammates' heads.

"All right! All right!" yelled Hank. Robbie gave Hank a raised fist.

Jay Manning threw another gopher ball. Robbie smoothly "tapped" it over the center-field fence! His teammates cheered and clapped. Robbie was telling himself, *That's right! Now I remember! It's all coming back to me!*

He hit six out of the next seven for sure extra-base hits. It was just like the old days—only better!

Ah, yes! he said to himself. *Right! Right! How could I ever have forgotten?*

Robbie looked around. The whole team as a group was smiling.

Chapter Ten

As the Redstone Colts' regular season came to a close, Robbie's batting slump did, too. Of course, he didn't start hitting in games as he had in batting practice, but his batting average climbed steadily. For the last ten games of the season, he batted over .600. Most of his hits were singles. His power hitting hadn't completely come back. But he still kept knocking in runs when they were needed.

Robbie's average went from under .200 to over .350 in just ten games. Frank Preston moved him up in the batting order to the cleanup spot. Jeff Streets moved down to fifth, with no hard feelings.

The line-up became:
  (1) Oscar Gonzales, SS (.290)
  (2) Hank Greengrass, CF (.360)

(3) Wally Potenza, RF (.322)
(4) Robbie Belmont, C (.350)
(5) Jeff Streets, 1B (.338)
(6) Lou Ranger, LF (.280)
(7) Tip Tyree, 3B (.282)
(8) Sidney Fisher, 2B (.277)
(9) Pitcher

Hank Greengrass's terrific average of .360 was deceptive. His hitting in the last ten games had been a dismal three-for-forty. His average used to be a lofty .450!

Hank's father, Gus, was now coming to every Redstone game, both home and away. Gus Greengrass even called Hank late at night with more batting suggestions and pep talks.

"I'm going nuts," Hank said to Robbie. "I have to start getting hits again just to make him leave me alone."

"Can you tell him not to come to any more games for a while? Or maybe Frank Preston could talk with him."

"I want to deal with family things inside the family if I can," said Hank. "But my father gets so angry so quickly. I'm afraid I'll set him off."

Now it became Robbie's turn to encourage Hank out of his slump. They tried to solve Hank's slump together as they had both solved Robbie's slump. They studied, discussed, and worked on Hank's batting. Robbie stayed after practice or came early to a game with Hank to do extra bat work. Hank began getting a few more hits, but nothing like before. They kept plugging away at the problem, hoping for a breakthrough.

Eagle changed from a temperamental showoff to an enthusiastic team player. He even sent Cynthia a decent, reasonable letter in which he apologized for all the bother he had caused her. Eagle promised in the letter not to do it anymore. Cynthia was so relieved when she got the letter that she cried a little. Robbie held her until she stopped.

Eagle was still tempted to throw temper tantrums. But Robbie could see him struggling successfully to stop himself from flying off the handle. By the fifty-ninth game of the season, Eagle had pitched seventeen straight innings without allowing a run. This was a team record. But then he hung a curve against a home-run hitter who blasted it out of the park. Eagle started to blame Robbie for calling for a curve, then realized it was his own fault for hanging it. His bad mood lasted only two more batters, both of whom Eagle walked.

Robbie went out to have a talk with him. Eagle said, "Sorry, Rob. I'm still mad for hanging that curve, I guess. It wasn't your fault, I know. I just lost interest in pitching tough to those batters."

"Keep practicing for your next perfect game,

Eagle," Robbie suggested. This put a glint back in Eagle's eye. He finished the game without allowing another runner to reach base.

The Redstone Colts were closing up the season with a pretty good record. Before the last regularly scheduled game, it stood at forty-two wins and seventeen losses. The Colts had faced a number of very talented teams all season—and beaten most of them. But they had also lost to some teams much weaker than they were.

Redstone's last game of the regular season was traditionally against the Mid-Tech Stars. The two were old rivals, and there had been some fierce contests in the past. Today's final game would be no exception. The selection committee for the post-season tournament usually took a set number of teams from each region in the country. Only one of these two teams was likely to be chosen by the committee for their region.

Mid-Tech's schedule had been easier than Redstone's. The Stars' record was forty-one wins and eighteen losses. But victory today at Redstone Stadium would give the Stars the same win-loss record as the Colts. And both teams knew today's winner would have a big advantage over the other in the minds of the selection committee.

Redstone Stadium was packed. Sitting among the fans for both teams were pro scouts who knew this might be their last chance to see Eagle Wilson pitch. Eagle was very excited about winning the hearts and contracts of the scouts. He was psyched up to pitch the game of his life. Robbie was a little worried that Eagle might be *too* wound up.

The game started with Eagle looking better than ever. His concentration was perfect. Each pitch he threw was like a little masterpiece.

Robbie had studied the scouting reports for the Mid-Tech Stars this season. During the week, he had gone over the videotape of their previous game. In addition, Robbie had closely watched the Stars take batting practice today. Scouting reports and old games can tell a catcher a lot about how opponents hit. But watching them on the day of the game gives the most up-to-date information about each batter.

Most of the Stars had the same batting strengths and weaknesses as before. But Robbie had noticed during batting practice which hitters had improved.

He knew their leadoff batter still liked to swing at slightly inside pitches. Eagle put two cutter fast balls and a crossfire pitch right at his fists. The batter obliged by striking out.

The second hitter was a tough guy named Roy Vetter. The scouting report on Vetter said to pitch him low balls. But in batting practice, Robbie had noticed Vetter creaming low balls all over the field and popping up high balls. Robbie signaled for a rising fast ball. Eagle shook the signal off, something he rarely did anymore.

Robbie thought for a second. He signaled again for the riser. Eagle glared for a moment, then nodded. Vetter swung at the riser and sent a routine fly ball out to Hank Greengrass in center field. As the infield threw the ball around, Eagle called softly to Robbie, "Good call."

Eagle struck out Mid-Tech's next hitter on three pitches, putting the ball exactly where Robbie asked for it.

"Way to look, Eagle!" Robbie said as he and Eagle trotted to the dugout together.

"Thanks, Robbie," Eagle said. He walked to the end of the bench to sit next to Wally Potenza. What they talked about, Robbie didn't know. But Eagle had been getting into the habit of sitting with Wally during games he was pitching. Wally had a calming effect on him. *All the better*, thought Robbie.

Pitching for Mid-Tech was Hal Hooper, called "Hoops" by his teammates. Hooper was an all-conference basketball player for Mid-Tech—and a super pitcher. He was a lanky left-hander with a whippy fast ball and an angry curve ball. He always had what seemed to be a surprised look on his face, as if every signal his catcher gave him was for a pitch he had never thrown before. It was a bit unnerving to bat against a pitcher who always looked as if he couldn't believe what was happening.

Redstone's leadoff batter, Oscar Gonzales, hit a weak grounder to first base for the first out. Hank Greengrass then came up and started to hit sharp fouls to the right. *He's hitting the ball well, but swinging late*, thought Robbie. Finally, Hank hit a grounder to the first baseman, who stepped on the bag for out number two.

"Swing at the ball, Hank! Don't slap at it!" Gus Greengrass called from his seat behind the home dugout.

Robbie entered the on-deck circle. "Good wood!" he said to Hank, who was just then passing by on his way to the dugout.

"Here," said Hank in frustration, "take my bat. There doesn't seem to be any more hits in that thing for me." Then Hank walked into the dugout. He didn't glance at all toward his father, who was calling out his name.

Robbie swung Hank's bat with his own, loosening up. He noticed that Hank's bat was at least two ounces heavier than his own. Robbie was still taking some practice swings when Wally Potenza struck out. The first inning was over, and Robbie went back into the dugout to put on his catching equipment.

Eagle kept up his spotless performance in the second inning. Three up, three down—he was looking unhittable. Again, he took his teammates' compliments in a mild way and sat himself down next to Wally in the dugout.

Robbie unbuckled his catching gear, then took his bat to the plate. The first pitch Robbie got was a straight fast ball on the outside corner for strike one. A low, inside curve ball was Hooper's second pitch.

Robbie kept cool, telling himself to hit it as if he were trying to tap a fly ball to a kid in the left-field bleachers. Robbie no longer had to pretend pitches were "bad" to hit them well. That gimmick had worked when he first broke out of his slump, but now it was a natural part of his normal swing again.

Robbie was easy and relaxed during his swing. Pitches now seemed to go slower than when he was uptight during his slump. He calmly watched the ball, which started to bend in toward him. A smile spread on Robbie's face as he swung. He felt he could actually *see* the ball hit his bat—it even seemed to flatten a bit at the point of impact. The ball flew to the left-field corner, where it bounced hard off the top of the fence.

Robbie sped around first base and tore for second. He heard Frank Preston yelling from third base, "Triple! Triple!" Robbie rounded second and sprinted to third. He gave it all he had. His batting helmet flew off his head as he went into his slide. The throw to third was a little wild. It hit his fallen batting helmet! The ball bounced crazily to the fence behind third base.

Robbie jumped up and legged it for home.

Mid-Tech's third baseman ran the ball down and threw it toward the plate. Robbie slid directly between the catcher's legs in a classic slide. In a cloud of dust, the umpire called Robbie safe.

A lengthy argument followed. The manager of the Stars said Robbie's batting helmet counted as part of Robbie, and so he had interfered with the ball. The umpire said no, that the ball had hit the helmet accidentally and, as such, was in play. Robbie's inside-the-park home run stood. The Colts went ahead, 1–0.

Chapter Eleven

Mid-Tech's Hal Hooper pitched shutout ball after Robbie's score, allowing only five more hits. Robbie had two of them and also stole two bases. But no one could drive him in. Hoops, with his surprised expression, bore down hard in the clutch. He doused every Redstone fire.

Eagle Wilson kept pitching beautifully, batter by batter, inning by inning. The fielding behind him was flawless. The team felt like a unit now. Everyone seemed satisfied with one another. Colt players chattered to one another, keeping themselves alert and sharp. Before each pitch, every Redstone fielder got set to have the ball hit in his direction. Eagle seemed to be able to sense when everyone was ready.

The Colt pitcher became more confident as the game went on. He looked as if he were made for the experience. When the top of the ninth inning came around, the Colts were still ahead, 1–0. The crowd was now on its feet, cheering Eagle even during his warm-up pitches. Eagle loved it. Though no one on the team said it aloud, Eagle was pitching a perfect game!

The first Mid-Tech batter in the ninth inning sliced a 2–1 curve over Jeff Streets's head and down the first-base line. But Wally Potenza had been running with the swing, showing good anticipation. At times during previous games, Wally had shown an uncanny talent for anticipating. But this was almost spooky. He caught the ball in the air two inches above the chalk on the right-field line. It was an unbelievable catch! Redstone fans went crazy, jumping up and down, stomping the stadium boards.

The next batter had been giving Eagle trouble the whole game. His name was Darrell Rhodes. Though he was Mid-Tech's number eight batter in the line-up, he was one of the few Stars to get good wood off Eagle two times in a row. He had hit Eagle's first pitch both times, so Robbie hadn't had a chance to learn much about him. The first pitch he had hit was low and inside. The other was high and outside. The scouting reports said that Darrell didn't *like* low, inside or high, outside pitches.

Since Rhodes might very well be swinging at the first pitch again, Robbie called for the nastiest pitch Eagle was throwing today: a fast, low,

113

outside curve ball. But Rhodes unloaded on this pitch, too! Robbie heard the heartbreaking sound of a mighty whack as Rhodes lined the ball between Eagle's legs before Eagle could get his glove down. Eagle fell to one knee and pounded the ground in frustration. He thought his perfect game was over.

But just then, Oscar Gonzales dived across the second-base bag and knocked the ball down with his glove. Sid Fisher was right there to pick the ball up. He zipped it to Jeff Streets, who was practically doing a split as he stretched for the throw.

"Out!" called the base umpire, throwing his thumb up in the air.

The home crowd went wild. The first-base coach for the Stars argued with the umpire. It had been a close play. Even Robbie wasn't sure about it until the umpire called the runner out.

"Way to go, Jeff!" Robbie shouted to Redstone's first baseman. "Nice stretch!"

"Thank Oscar and Sid," Jeff said, looking at his fellow infielders. "They were the ones who pulled it off."

Oscar and Sid smiled at each other as they returned to their positions. Redstone's fans continued to applaud. As they did, Robbie decided to have a quick chat with Eagle.

"You okay?" asked Robbie.

"Yeah," said Eagle. "Just give me a second to get composed."

"You take as much time as you want, Eagle."

The next Mid-Tech batter was the pitcher, Hal Hooper. *Hope he's the last batter*, thought Robbie. Hooper was a good-hitting pitcher. He was batting .326 for the year. Eagle had struck him out once on a change-up curve ball. The other time, Hoops had grounded out on a cutter fast ball.

Eagle took his time. He went to the rosin bag. He took his hat off and wiped his brow. He tugged at the sleeves of his undershirt. He fixed up the mound just right. Finally, he was ready.

With the crowd chanting "Eagle, Eagle, Eagle!" and "Hoops, Hoops, Hoops!" with each pitch, the count went to two balls and two strikes. Robbie then called for a cutter.

Eagle shook him off.

Now? Robbie wondered. *He picks this time to disagree?*

Robbie repeated the sign for the cutter. Eagle shook it off again. Robbie called time and went out to talk with him.

"What gives, Eagle?" he asked.

"I want to go with the change-up curve. I got this guy out with it in the third, remember?"

"Yeah, I remember. But we both know it's a lot harder fooling a batter with the same change-up a second time. I think we should go with the cutter here."

"Hey, who's pitching—you or me? I say we go with the change-up curve. I know I can fool this guy with it again."

"Okay, okay. Change-up curve it is." Robbie returned to the plate and squatted behind it for the next pitch.

Eagle was right. It fooled Hooper again. He was way out in front of the slow, slippery curve. Off-balance, he swung weakly at the pitch that was heading for the strike zone. His bat ticked the underbelly of the ball. It looped toward short left-center.

Four fielders tore like mad for the slowly falling ball: Oscar and Sidney from the infield, and Lou Ranger and Hank Greengrass from the outfield. The ball touched the ground a half second before Oscar's diving glove reached the spot.

Hooper, a very fast runner, rounded first base. His eyes bugged out even more when he saw that no one was covering second base. He raced to second. The Colts' third baseman, Tip Tyree, sprinted to cover second. The throw came from Hank Greengrass. It was too late.

But Hoops didn't stop. No one was covering third base now! So Mid-Tech's pitcher tore for third. Robbie ran to cover it. As he charged toward third, he saw Eagle standing on the mound, gaping as if in a daze.

"Eagle!" Robbie yelled. "Cover home!"

Eagle snapped to attention. Robbie didn't have

116

time to see if Eagle actually did run in to cover the plate. Robbie, Tip's throw, and Hooper were all converging on third base at the same time.

Hooper won the race by a foot. And he didn't stop this time, either.

Robbie caught the ball while running toward third. His momentum carried him a few yards toward left field. He put on the brakes and pivoted, ready to throw the ball home.

But Eagle was just now running in to cover the plate! Robbie threw the ball slower than he normally would, leading Eagle as a quarterback would a receiver. The throw arrived knee-high at the plate the moment Eagle did. He caught it cleanly and smoothly, then swept the tag into Hooper's sliding spikes. "Out!" yelled the plate umpire.

The game was over! The Redstone Colts had won, 1–0! They seemed certain to go on to the regional tournament!

In the locker room after the game, the Colts were celebrating loudly. Only Eagle remained in a funk. He sat in front of his locker, with his shirt off, not moving. He had missed a perfect game by one stupid pitch. He couldn't believe that it was his own fault.

When Robbie passed his locker, Eagle complained that Robbie should've gone along with his change-up idea more. "If you hadn't resisted so much, I would have been more confident, thrown a better pitch."

"Eagle, we won. And besides, the scouts couldn't help but be impressed, even if it wasn't a perfect game. A bloop single—that's all you gave up. You're going to be a first-round draft choice, man!"

Eagle again spoke in a dead voice. "If you hadn't fought the idea, I'd have thrown a better pitch."

Robbie was now annoyed. "Look, if you had taken my sign as you did for every other pitch, you'd probably have your second perfect game now!"

Eagle stood up. His face was red. "Oh, yeah, I keep forgetting that you're Mister Know-It-All. Everything you do, every call, turns out right, huh?"

"I didn't say that, Eagle. You did. I make mistakes just like anyone else." Robbie saw a few teammates staring at the two bickering players. "Say, could we put this behind us? I mean, we *did* win, right? We should be celebrating!"

"Yeah, we won," Eagle said dully. "Whoop-dee-do."

"Eagle, I'm really sorry you didn't get a perfect game today. I mean it. Do you believe me?"

"Sure, Belmont. Who wouldn't believe Mister Know-It-All?"

Not this again, thought Robbie sadly. *Please, let's not go through this again!*

A half hour later, Robbie was talking with Cynthia in the parking lot. Eagle passed by, walking slowly by himself.

"Oh, hi, Cynthia," he said as he passed.

"Hi, Eagle," said Robbie. "Is your car around here?"

"I was speaking to Cynthia, not you, Belmont!" Eagle snapped.

"Hi, Eagle," said Cynthia finally. "Everything okay?"

"Sure—if just missing a perfect game can be called okay!"

"I know. I saw the ball float down just before Oscar could get to it. I'm really sorry."

Suddenly, Eagle's face turned from anger to hurt. Robbie almost swore he could see Eagle's eyes mist up. *Boy, you know just what buttons to push, guy, don't you?* thought Robbie.

"What am I going to do, Cynth?" Eagle asked almost in a pout.

Robbie had had enough. "Come off it, Eagle! You're just trying to win Cynthia's sympathy here. And it won't wash!"

"Robbie!" said Cynthia in surprise.

"Oh, come on, Cynthia. You're not going to fall for this, are you?"

"Hey, I'll leave you two alone," said Eagle,

slowly moving off. "I don't want Cynthia disobeying her boyfriend or anything."

"Wait, Eagle," said Cynthia. Then she spoke to Robbie in a whisper. "I know it's a line. But he *is* hurting a bit. I can tell. And I can help. I'll just get a cup of coffee with him. That's all. To cheer him up. Call me in an hour, okay? Trust me."

Before Robbie could reply, she was next to Eagle. The two walked off toward his car. Robbie noticed how much faster Eagle was now walking.

In disgust, Robbie threw his duffel bag as far as he could across the asphalt.

Chapter Twelve

Robbie called Cynthia after an hour, and she *was* there. Cynthia told Robbie her cup of coffee with Eagle helped him feel better. Robbie was thinking, *Well, okay. If Eagle feels better, that's good for the team*. Then Cynthia told him she would probably have coffee again with him some time.

"Too much coffee is bad for you," said Robbie.

"What does that mean—my seeing Eagle is bad for me?"

"I think Eagle is partly faking how hurt he is. It's his way of getting you back again."

"He won't win me back, Robbie. I'm sure of it."

"Aha! I knew one day you'd be sure!"

"I've been sure for a while, Robbie," she said over the phone.

Robbie was happy to hear it. He knew he had to trust her and *should* trust her.

Eagle kept coming up with reasons to get together with Cynthia. She helped him study history. She also calmed him down when he complained about some body ache that might end his pitching career. And she hung out with him occasionally when Wally Potenza wasn't around and Eagle wanted company. Cynthia told Robbie she was working out a friendship with Eagle after breaking up with him as a boyfriend.

As Cynthia and Eagle were finding a way to be friends, Robbie and Eagle were slipping back into their old tension. This became obvious during Redstone's first regional tournament game, which was against the Slater University Terriers at a ballpark just thirty miles from Redstone itself. It was bad enough when any two players on a team felt very cool toward each other. But when a catcher and a pitcher felt that way, it couldn't help but affect the game. There were little breaks in the working rhythm between Eagle and Robbie. Those often led to poor pitches, which Terrier batters gratefully slammed all over the field.

Going into the ninth inning, Slater was ahead of Redstone, 6–5. All five Colt runs came off Robbie's bat. His three crisp hits drove in five base runners.

But it was Charlie Diskin who tied the game in the ninth. Pinch-hitting for Eagle, Charlie ripped a fast ball into the left-field bleachers for a solo home run. The whole Redstone bench stood and cheered him as he circled the bases.

Oscar Gonzales left the on-deck circle for home plate. Hank Greengrass grabbed his bat and was about to step out of the dugout for the on-deck circle when Robbie tugged his sleeve.

"How heavy is that bat of yours?" Robbie asked him.

"Why?"

"You're swinging late," answered Robbie.

"This is the same weight my dad swung when he was at Redstone, so I figured it'd be good enough for me."

"You're not your dad, Hank," Robbie said gently. "Try a lighter bat."

Hank thought about what Robbie said, then shook his head. "I'll stick to the one I have, Robbie. Thanks anyway." He headed for the on-deck circle.

After fouling off three straight pitches, Oscar Gonzales brought the crowd to its feet with a smash double down the left-field line. Hank Greengrass now came to bat.

"Haul off on one, Hank!" his father called out.

Hank cracked a shot foul into the right-field stands—another late swing. Hank stepped out of the box and tightened his batting gloves. He looked bothered. Then he choked up on the bat and stepped into the box.

"No choking!" yelled Gus Greengrass from his seat behind Redstone's dugout. "No choking!"

Robbie saw Hank's shoulders sag. *He thinks his dad's telling him not to blow it*, thought Robbie. *Hank doesn't realize his dad meant "don't choke up," not "don't choke."*

Hank took a deep breath and fixed his eyes on the pitcher. A snapping curve ball came in, and Hank swung on it. He hit it flush, and the ball sailed up the middle for a clean single. Oscar scooted home with the winning run. Despite Eagle's poor pitching, the Colts had pulled the game out, 7–6.

Jubilant, the Redstone team filed into the locker room—except Hank. He was standing by the front railing near the dugout. His father was talking to him angrily. As Robbie trailed into the locker room, he overheard part of what Gus was saying to his son. "Don't ever choke up again. You hear me? That's telling the pitcher you can't get around on his pitches. Show no weakness at the plate. None."

Robbie and Cynthia spent a lot of their time together talking about her and Eagle. On one hand, Robbie was glad they talked, because it helped relieve his jealousy. On the other hand, Robbie didn't like talking about Eagle so much. It made Eagle too important, which was just what Robbie didn't want as far as Cynthia was concerned. Cynthia told him often that she liked Eagle as a friend and nothing more. Robbie said, *"You* may think that, but Eagle doesn't."

When the season began, it was Eagle hating Robbie, with Robbie trying to calm Eagle down. Now it was Robbie feeling anything but friendly toward Eagle. And Eagle wasn't doing anything to calm Robbie down. Outside of brief hellos and baseball talk, they hardly said anything to each other.

Redstone's second regional tournament game was against the Haven University Schooners, a strong team. Robbie knocked in his ninety-second and ninety-third RBI's for the season in the last inning to win the game, 5–4. Clem Goodall started, and his well-practiced splitter held the opponents to three runs in eight innings. Roger Conklin's fast ball was slower than usual in relief, and his twin had to save him in the ninth. It was a good team effort that won the game. The tension between Eagle and Robbie had no chance to ruin it.

Hank Greengrass went back to not choking up on the bat. He had gone hitless in four at-bats. When Robbie asked him why he didn't choke up, Hank just said, "Because that's not how my dad did it." Hank walked away before Robbie could reply.

Eagle Wilson started the third regional tournament game for Redstone. He came into the game with a record of 19–7. Only two pitchers in major college baseball history had ever won twenty games in a single season. Eagle had the chance to become the third. And yet he and Robbie didn't speak more than ten words to each other before the game.

The Colts' opponents were the number-one pick to win the regional, the Skyler University Bears. Their second, third, and fourth batters were known as "the Bermuda Triangle." That's because pitches thrown to these three seemed to disappear. They were awesome sluggers, each batting over .350. Their names together sounded like a law firm of wrestlers: Wrango, Stretch, and Pound.

The scouting report Robbie had on these guys was not all that much help. It recommended a low ball to Pete Wrango because he rested his bat flat on his shoulder. This type of batting stance makes it easier to hit high balls but harder to hit low ones. At least, that's the theory. Wrango punched a hole in the theory when he punched Eagle's first knee-high cutter fast ball down the left-field line. It hit the wall on two hops for a double.

The scouting report on Jim Stretch, the second member of "the Bermuda Triangle," said that if he had any weakness, it was swinging at bad balls. The only problem was, Stretch not only swung at bad balls, but also plastered them.

He cracked a pitchout into the gap between right and center field for the second Skyler double of the day.

On the Bears' cleanup batter, Jefferson Pound, the scouting report had only two words: "Good luck." Pound had no known batting weaknesses. Robbie watched carefully when Pound took batting practice. Robbie couldn't see any weakness, either! Pound had a beautiful swing. He could hit anything for power and swung only at strikes.

Robbie signaled for unusual pitches to Pound, hoping to break his concentration somehow. But the heavyset giant clubbed a crossfire curve into the left-field bleachers for a home run. The Bears were ahead, 3–0, in the first inning!

It was a hard blow to Redstone's morale. The players hung their heads a little and scraped the ground with their spikes. Robbie went to the mound to say something encouraging to Eagle. But once he got there, he couldn't think of anything to say!

The two just stood there. Neither said a word. Even Oscar Gonzales didn't join them. No one wanted to be around the feuding catcher and pitcher these days.

Finally, Eagle said, "What'd you come out here for if you've got nothing to say?"

Robbie turned around and went back to his position. When the next Bear batter came up, the chatter around Redstone's infield was weak and forced.

The rest of Skyler's hitters were not nearly as fearsome as "the Bermuda Triangle." But Eagle was so rattled that he gave up two more runs before the first inning ended. Robbie was unable to help him. No one on the team could make him confident again.

The next time Wrango, Stretch, and Pound came up, more runs scored. Coach Preston replaced Eagle with Roger Conklin in the sixth inning. The Colts were behind, 7–1. The lone Redstone run was scored in the fourth inning. Robbie smacked a double that sent Wally Potenza home from second base.

Roger Conklin couldn't do much better than Eagle. Nor could Wyatt when he replaced his brother in the ninth inning. The Colts' morale was at its lowest point now. Robbie managed a solo homer in the ninth, but it was too little too late. The Skyler Bears humiliated the Redstone Colts, 13–2.

Hank Greengrass had still held his heavy bat at the very bottom of the handle. He forced himself to step earlier so his swing could get around on time. It made him look a little awkward at the plate, but he at least got one hit, a single to right-center field.

Robbie tried to talk with Hank after the game.

But he said, "No discussion. I got a hit today. So the problem is solved."

Fortunately, it was a double-elimination tournament. Only teams that lost twice were out of it. The Colts could still win the regional tournament if they won all their remaining games in it. But team spirit was low. The Colts didn't feel like a unit anymore. And the chances of beating the remaining tournament teams, all strong, seemed especially bleak.

Robbie believed his poor communication with Eagle was at the heart of the Colts' slumping morale.

"I agree," Cynthia said to Robbie one evening during dinner in the Redstone cafeteria. "For a while, I thought I could *make* Eagle talk with you. I can't, of course. You know, even our friendship has gotten rocky lately. He gets into these awful moods."

Robbie nodded. Cynthia picked up her knife and tapped her plate with it softly. She seemed lost in thought.

"I've decided not to hang out with Eagle anymore. Even as friends." Cynthia laid the knife on her plate and looked at Robbie. "You were right. Now I only hope this doesn't make things worse for everybody."

"I don't see how it could," said Robbie. "And who knows? Maybe this is the jolt Eagle needs."

So Cynthia told Eagle they wouldn't be hanging out anymore. Eagle just looked at her. It was as if a light had been switched off inside him.

Clem Goodall pitched the next regional tournament game for the Colts—and threw a shutout! His splitter had finally come into its own. With that pitch and a slow, late-breaking curve, Clem showed what kind of pitcher he could be. The Colt sophomore made a strong impression on everyone—teammates, opponents, and scouts alike.

Hank Greengrass went hitless. His joy in the team's victory was offset by his father's criticism of his day at the plate.

Then the news came that the Haven University Schooners had eked out a victory over the Skyler Bears! The schedule demanded that Haven and Skyler play each other again in the next game, the regional semifinal. The Redstone Colts had to play the Dalton College Buccaneers in the other semifinal.

Even though Cynthia wasn't seeing Eagle anymore, Robbie felt the situation hadn't really improved. Then Eagle's bad mood started to lighten after a week. Wally Potenza had been spending a lot of time with Eagle. This time around, it didn't take Wally as long to calm him down. Robbie was also feeling less angry toward Eagle.

For some reason, everybody seemed to be having personal problems at this time. Brian Webster hadn't been talking with Joshua Kenny for over a month because Joshua had been going out with Dori again without writing Melinda about it. Brian had told Joshua he thought it was wrong. Joshua had told him to mind his own business. And Robbie knew from letters Melinda had written to him that she had been dating Terry Lioni. Josh knew nothing about it!

Robbie tried to ease the strain between Brian and Joshua, and he made some progress. But between Robbie and Eagle, Wally Potenza was the peacemaker.

Wally finally got Robbie and Eagle together a few nights before Redstone's semifinal with the Dalton Buccaneers. All three of them got some ice-cream cones and walked around the campus eating them. They talked about how they had to forget their personal problems on the field. Wally ended by saying, "Don't forget. You two are one heck of a battery when you're plugged into each other."

Eagle looked off, then turned and said, "Let's start over again, Robbie. Tell Cynthia I'm sorry for not trying to understand. I'll be all right from here on. I promise. Cynthia and I will talk again someday. Can you see something like that happening?"

"Sure," said Robbie.

"Good," said Eagle, smiling.

They shook hands.

"Ow," said Eagle, grabbing his own shoulder.

"What?" asked Robbie and Wally at the same time.

"I don't know," Eagle said. "Some little twinge in my arm. It's gone now . . . I think." He felt delicately around his shoulder for any more twinges.

Robbie broke into laughter. Eagle looked at him crossly, but Wally laughed, too.

"What?" said Eagle.

"I forgot how much I like you, Eags," Robbie said, starting to clap Eagle on the back. Robbie's hand stopped in midair, then very slowly came down and patted Eagle's back with exaggerated care. "Whoops, sorry. I hope I didn't just give you another twinge."

Eagle nodded. With a little smile he said, "I guess I do tend to complain about aches every now and then."

"You go right ahead, Eagle," Wally said.

"Take care of that golden arm," said Robbie. "We're going to need it for the Buccaneers."

Eagle was terrific against the Dalton Buccaneers. He pitched a perfect game for three innings, a no-hitter for five innings, a shutout for seven innings, and a three-hit, 3–1 victory in nine innings.

Robbie felt the old rhythm working with Eagle again. He called for the same kind of pitches, but somehow they all came in with something extra on the ball. That "extra" was teamwork.

The whole team felt they were back in a groove again. Robbie went three-for-four at the plate, knocking in all three runs for Redstone.

Only Hank Greengrass seemed out of it. He was not talking with anyone lately, even Robbie. Hank only had one hit in five at-bats. It was a single to left field off of a change-up.

The Skyler Bears-Haven Schooners game followed theirs. All the Colts watched. Robbie sat next to Joshua Kenny.

During the course of the game, Joshua told Robbie, "I'm thinking of writing Melinda a letter telling her everything Brian said I should."

"That would turn out better than you think, old pal," said Robbie.

"What's that supposed to mean?"

"It just means you can't go wrong being honest with someone like Melinda," said Robbie.

"How do you know?" asked Joshua.

Robbie could see Joshua believed him. "The same way you know," Robbie answered.

Joshua didn't say anything back. But Robbie figured Josh would probably call Melinda that night.

Meanwhile, the Bears crushed the Schooners, 12–3. The "Bermuda Triangle" never looked stronger. They accounted for nine of Skyler's dozen runs. The Colts were going to have their hands more than full for the regional final in a few days.

Chapter Thirteen

In the Redstone Colts' locker room before their regional tournament final against the Skyler Bears, Robbie felt something was wrong. He couldn't quite put his finger on it, but the mood wasn't right.

He himself felt ready and psyched up. But the other Colts seemed *too* calm. The jokes they made seemed too relaxed to Robbie. They talked about Wrango, Stretch, and Pound as if they were characters out of Greek mythology, with powers beyond the reach of mere college players.

This made Robbie a little angry, but he wasn't sure why. He didn't say anything. He didn't want to foul up people's moods. He chattered encouragingly. Usually, this got similar chatter in response. But this time it just caused some half-baked chatter or even a surprised look. It was strange.

Clem Goodall started for Redstone. Eagle had pitched so recently that his arm was still tired. But if needed, he would be ready to relieve Clem in the early innings.

The Colts were designated the home team, so they took the field first defensively. Clem struck out the first Skyler batter on three straight splitters. He looked as if he had good control over this modern version of the fork ball. Robbie was even getting high hopes that the splitter could put the "Bermuda Triangle" on ice.

But Pete Wrango teed off on the splitter even as it dipped nastily. He didn't just hit it—he mauled it. The ball shot between Lou Ranger and Hank Greengrass. Wrango ended up on third base.

The triple seemed to shatter Clem's confidence in his splitter. Wrango had hit one of the best splitters Clem had ever thrown! Clem shook off Robbie's call for a splitter against Jim Stretch. Robbie called for it again. He wanted it thrown very low and outside since Stretch would swing at bad pitches. Clem nodded and went into a half stretch. But he threw a very slow splitter that hardly dropped at all and came down the middle of the plate.

Stretch clubbed the fat pitch over Wally Potenza's head in right field for another triple. It was just like the last game—only worse! Clem was badly shaken. All the Colt fielders were quiet.

No shouts of encouragement came from the Redstone bench except Frank Preston's. He was clapping his hands and shouting, "Okay! Okay! Stay on top of this! Heads-up ball!"

Robbie walked out to the mound to give Clem a little time to settle his nerves. The two didn't say much. Robbie just reminded him to shake off the last hit and make every new pitch count. He told Clem to be careful not to tighten his arm up when he threw the splitter. After a minute, Robbie trotted back to the catcher's box. "One out!" he yelled, holding up his index finger for all the fielders to see. "Infielders in! Get the runner at home if you can!"

"There are no outs, Robbie," said Clem from the mound.

"One out, Clem. You struck out the first batter! You can do it! Heads up!"

He didn't even know how many outs there were! thought Robbie. *Sheesh!*

The infielders moved in closer to improve their chances of getting the lead runner at the plate. Normally, they wouldn't have to be reminded of this, but this time Robbie needed to wake them up. *It's as if everyone's hypnotized!* he thought.

Skyler cleanup slugger Jefferson Pound was up. Robbie still hadn't figured out a good pitching strategy against him. *Let's see what he does with the splitter,* Robbie thought. Again, Clem shook it off.

Robbie called time and hustled out for another conference. He told Clem that Pound could hit any other pitch, but maybe not the splitter. "Keep your arm loose and throw it the way I know you can," Robbie said. Clem took a deep breath and nodded.

Jefferson Pound did have trouble with the splitter. He still hit it hard, but on the ground. It went right to Oscar Gonzales, who was in closer than usual at shortstop. He gloved the ball cleanly and tossed it to Robbie in the nick of time to nab Stretch sliding home.

"All right!" Robbie called, throwing the ball back to Clem. "Way to pitch, Clem! Way to go, Oscar! Two outs now! Play's at first!" Robbie was glad to hear a little more life in the fielders as they chattered and got ready for the next batter.

But the fifth Bear batter lined a double down the left-field line off a good curve. Robbie could see the gloom settle again on his teammates. They thought they were out of the fire after getting past "the Bermuda Triangle." But the fifth batter had hit the ball hard. And Clem served a tight-armed fast ball to the sixth batter, who knocked a single to left field. Another run scored. It was now 2–0, Skyler.

Jay Manning came out and had a conference with Clem, Robbie, and Oscar. Clem said he felt okay, although there was a confused look in his eyes. Eagle had started to warm up in the bull-pen, but he wasn't ready yet. Jay decided to leave Clem in.

Clem threw some poor pitches to the seventh Bear hitter, who finally hauled off on a splitter that didn't sink. The ball flew straight and deep to center field. Hank Greengrass tore after it.

As he did, Robbie heard a fan shout "No! No! No!" over and over, louder and louder. It was Gus Greengrass.

After a long run, Hank caught the ball a few yards in front of the wall. The crowd gave him a nice hand for catching the third out. As Robbie trotted back to the dugout, he saw Gus Greengrass stumbling toward the exit and out of the stands.

I guess he thought Hank was going to hit the center-field wall—just as he did to end his career! Robbie thought. *Gus is trying to live out the rest of his career through his son!*

The mood in the Colts' dugout was somber in their half of the first inning. Robbie tried to talk up some spirit, but was met with dazed looks.

Skyler's number two pitcher was starting, a bearded senior named Buzz Petroff. Oscar hit an 0–2 pitch weakly back to Buzz for the first out. Afterward, Oscar said to his teammates in the dugout that he couldn't understand why Petroff was their number *two* pitcher. "His fast ball has a lot more action on it than their number one pitcher," he said, recalling the last time Redstone played Skyler. "And this guy's curve breaks later."

This did nothing to help the Colts' morale.

Hank Greengrass seemed unsteady at the plate. When he stepped out of the box, he looked into the stands where his father was supposed to be. Hank struck out on five pitches. As he passed Robbie in the on-deck circle, Hank said Petroff's curve was unhittable. Robbie nearly spit. *No one is unhittable!* he thought to himself.

Wally Potenza tried a surprise bunt with two strikes on him. But he bunted it foul for strike three. The inning was over.

Robbie went back to the dugout and put his catcher's equipment on. Besides the shin guards, chest protector, and mask, Robbie wore a catcher's helmet. It was like a batting helmet with no brim. He also wore a skin glove under his catcher's glove.

As Robbie was putting on his gear, Wally came by. "I bunted," he said to Robbie, "because I didn't think I could hit him."

What is wrong with this picture? Robbie thought.

In the second inning, Clem Goodall retired the Bears one-two-three. Robbie led off the second inning for the Colts with a crisp single to left field off Buzz Petroff's late-breaking curve. *He's hittable!* Robbie thought to himself. "Come on, Jeff!" he called to Jeff Streets, Redstone's next batter. "Your pitcher! Your pitcher!"

On Buzz Petroff's third pitch, Robbie took off

139

for second. It was a hit-and-run play. Jeff slammed a Petroff fast ball, but it went right into Jim Stretch's glove at shortstop. Stretch threw it to Pete Wrango at first base, easily doubling Robbie off. Then Lou Ranger took a called third strike to end the second inning. The Colts' spirit had flared up briefly after Robbie's hit, but now it seemed dead again.

The "Bermuda Triangle" led off the third inning for the Skyler Bears. Pete Wrango whammed a crossfire curve off the right-field wall for a double.

Man, can these guys hit! Robbie thought. Obviously, his teammates were thinking the same thing. As Jim Stretch stepped into the batter's box, Robbie could almost *hear* his teammates thinking: *Here we go again!*

That fear got greater after Stretch hit the first pitch for home-run distance but three feet foul. Coach Frank Preston called time and headed out to the mound, waving for Eagle Wilson to come in. The confused look was still in Clem's eyes. Robbie thought it was a good time for a new pitcher.

Eagle said his arm felt a little stiff. Robbie reminded Eagle there would be lots of time for his arm to recover after this game.

After Eagle's warm-up pitches, Jim Stretch stepped back into the batter's box. Eagle threw him a sailer fast ball a foot outside. Robbie had asked for the ball that far outside, knowing Stretch would go after fishballs.

Stretch did go after it—and sent a screaming shot down the third-base line! It was another double, scoring Skyler's third run. It didn't seem to matter who was pitching for Redstone. Eagle shook his head sadly, almost smiling. Robbie didn't like that.

Eagle threw a beautiful set of pitches to Jefferson Pound, working the count to 1–2. Then he threw his best pitch yet, a fast-sinking curve on the low, inside corner. But Jefferson Pound swatted it over the center-field wall for a home run!

The Bears were now leading 5–0 in the top of the third inning with no outs. It looked like a rout. Eagle was shaking his head again. This time he *was* smiling, as if saying, "What can you do? These guys are hitting everything."

Eagle walked the next batter on five pitches. To Robbie's eyes, giving up a walk didn't seem to bother Eagle as much as it should. Then, on the fourth pitch to the next batter, Eagle forgot he had a man on base and took a full wind-up! The batter swung and missed.

It took the runner on first base a second to realize what Eagle was doing. That allowed just enough time for Robbie to peg the ball exactly to the second-base bag, catching the runner by a hair.

The play seemed to perk the Colts up. Getting

the runner had wiped out Eagle's mistake of taking a full wind-up with a man on. Eagle struck out the batter and got the next one to hit a blooper to right field. Wally Potenza made a nice running catch of the ball.

Robbie jogged back to the dugout and noticed that a lot of the Colt fielders were running in with a tired look. Some were even moping. No one said anything about getting some runs. There was hardly any chatter at all. The players sat quietly on the bench, whispering to each other in small groups. *That's what this team used to do in the beginning of the season*, Robbie thought, *before we became a unit*.

Tip Tyree, Redstone's third baseman, hit an easy pop-up to Skyler's second baseman. There was no particular reaction from the Colts' dugout. The whispered conversations went on undisturbed. Walking the length of the dugout to get a drink of water, Robbie overheard bits and pieces of those conversations.

"We can't get by that Bermuda Triangle without losing something!"

"Any plans for a summer job?"

"All in all, we've had a pretty good season. This can't change that."

"My girlfriend and I were going to celebrate with the team, but now we'll just have a nice romantic dinner. That's even better in some ways!"

"We can't stop them from scoring on us, and we can't get any hits against Petroff. He's too good today!"

Robbie was getting angrier and angrier with each bit of conversation he heard. Even Joshua Kenny and Brian Webster, Redstone's student assistants, were talking about what kind of team the Colts would have next year.

"With Eagle gone, Clem will be our starter," said Joshua.

Robbie was happy that his two friends were now speaking to each other again. But he couldn't stand what they were talking about at that moment.

Brian said to Joshua, "And Hank and Robbie will be back."

Suddenly, Robbie could take no more. "All right, you guys," he said, louder than usual.

The entire dugout grew quiet and looked at him.

"We still have a chance to win this game, right?" Robbie continued.

Frank Preston was about to say something, then decided to stay silent. Robbie took that to mean he should go on.

"Look, I'm not good at this rah-rah stuff. But if *they* can score five runs on us, *we* can score five runs on them. And more."

At that point, Sidney Fisher, number eight in

the Colts' line-up, hit an easy one back to the pitcher for the second out.

"Okay, the guy's a good pitcher," Robbie went on. "That's why we should be studying him like crazy in these early innings. The more we know, the quicker we'll start chipping away at him."

Just then, Eagle hit an easy one back to the pitcher for the third out. But Robbie would not be stopped. The players all listened to him, as if hearing something they had forgotten but wanted badly to remember.

"From here on, we shut them down cold," said Robbie. "Not one more run, not an inch."

Eagle had come back to the dugout after his at-bat. He was surprised that none of the Colt players had taken the field yet.

"No more runs, Eagle!" said Robbie, looking directly at him now. "A perfect game to the end! If you've been wondering what the scouts think of you, try getting the Bermuda Triangle out every time they come up to the plate. *That* will get the scouts' attention!"

Oscar Gonzales, Redstone's captain, stood up, walked to the middle of the dugout, and put out his hand. "Team!" he shouted.

All the other players and the coaches huddled around him, placing their hands on top of his. "Team!" they shouted with him. "Team! Team!"

Then, with a roar, they broke from the huddle. The starters raced out to the field, with their teammates clapping and yelling encouragement from the dugout. As Robbie snapped on his catching gear and started for home plate, he passed Frank Preston. The coach ran his hand through his hair under his cap—and smiled.

Chapter Fourteen

Eagle Wilson pitched like a new man. It was "Perfect Game" Wilson again. Six pitches and three crisp fielding plays retired the Skyler Bears in order. The Colts sprinted in from their positions. The chatter in the dugout was determined and full of energy. Redstone fans in the stadium picked up on it. They started clapping and chanting for their Colts. Robbie could hear Cynthia Wu's voice, calling out with the others.

"Where did my father go?" Hank asked Robbie.

"He left after you caught that fly ball close to the wall in the first inning. He seemed afraid you were going to kill yourself running into the wall."

"Or end my career," Hank said wryly.

"Hank, we need *you* up there, not your dad."

Hank sighed. "I know, I know," he said. There was a pause. "I hate that heavy bat if you want to know the truth," Hank said. He looked at the bat Robbie held. "Your bat's lighter. I've always liked it."

With a grin, Robbie held out his bat toward Hank.

"You sure about this?" asked Hank, not taking it.

"I'm sure," said Robbie. "Come on, take it."

Smiling, Hank took the bat and walked to the on-deck circle.

Oscar Gonzales stepped in the batter's box as if he meant to make up for lost time quickly. As team captain, Oscar wanted to start off a rally to inspire his team back into the game.

Oscar waited Petroff out, working the count to 2–2. He wanted mainly to get on base. That was the leadoff man's job, and he was determined to do it.

Buzz Petroff's next pitch slipped out of his hand as he pitched it. It sailed way over Oscar's head. Thinking quickly, Oscar swung at it as it passed, knowing he wouldn't hit it. After swinging, he tore for first base!

The wild pitch sailed past the catcher. It was strike three, but the catcher hadn't caught the pitch. That meant the catcher had to chase after the ball and throw Oscar out at first to get him out.

Oscar made it to first in plenty of time. He had taken the strikeout in order to gain the base.

Team spirit! The captain had asserted himself. Redstone players were on the top step of the dugout, cheering Oscar's quick thinking.

Skyler's manager and coaches were arguing loudly with the umpire. "He swung at it on purpose, ump!" fumed the manager. "He can't intentionally miss the ball!"

The umpire shouted back, "Can, too! Batter can choose to swing as the ball passes!"

Finally, the Bears accepted the umpire's call, and the game went on.

"Come on, Hank!" Robbie shouted as Hank Greengrass stepped in the box. "We'll show them our own Bermuda Triangle—you, Wally, and me!"

"Triangle?" said Jeff Streets, who batted fifth in Redstone's line-up. "What about me? You mean Bermuda *Quadrangle,* don't you, Robbie?"

"Hey, don't leave me out of this!" blurted Lou Ranger, the Colts' sixth batter.

Then the whole bench got into the act.

"Okay, okay," said Robbie, smiling. "I guess you could say we have *all* the angles covered today. You guys are something else!"

Robbie took his place in the on-deck circle. From there, he noticed that Gus Greengrass had returned to his seat. Hank noticed, too. *At least Gus won't see his son choking up on the bat!* thought Robbie.

Hank worked the count to two balls and one strike. He was no longer stepping early. Hank

148

had gone back to the stance he used when he was hitting at a fantastic clip in the first part of the season. He smacked the next Petroff pitch foul into the left-field stands. Then, Hank got hold of a curve ball and ripped it down the left-field line for a double! This was clearly a different Hank from the one who had called Petroff unhittable in the first inning. Oscar, scampering like a crazy greyhound, scored all the way from first. The Colts were finally on the scoreboard, 5–1.

In the first inning, Wally Potenza had thought the only way he could get a hit off Petroff was by bunting with two strikes. Now, he calmly stepped right into the first Petroff pitch. His aluminum bat clanged it right back into Petroff's mitt in the blink of an eye. The smart pitcher didn't waste any time marveling at his luck. He whirled and picked off Hank Greengrass, who was diving too late back to second.

Robbie clapped his hands and shouted encouragement to Wally and Hank, who were frustrated by how the play turned out. "Great contact, Wally! You'll get more chances. Chin up, Hank! Not your fault."

"Show them where you live, Robbie!" Hank said, starting to hustle off the field.

"Keep it going, Robbie," said Wally. "Keep us alive now!"

Robbie took a called first strike that he thought

was outside. *College umpires have a very generous strike zone,* Robbie reflected. Petroff's next pitch was a hopping, high fast ball. It looked just fine to Robbie. He slugged it *over* the center-field wall and beyond the runway behind the wall! It was a monstrous stroke. Redstone fans were actually hushed for a second before they broke into cheers. Even Skyler's fans applauded the hit.

The Colts didn't score any more runs that inning. And in the top of the fourth inning, Eagle had to face Wrango, Stretch, and Pound.

"Perfect game, Eagle!" Robbie called, thumping his mitt. "Every pitch!" Wrango's huge form stepped in the box, casting a shadow over Robbie. "I want to see something special, Eags! Show me the best now!" Robbie called, as he gave Eagle a signal for a low, cutter fast ball.

Robbie wanted Eagle to reach back for that special extra on each pitch. Throughout the season, Robbie had seen Eagle display a rare quality most great pitchers had. It was sensing what the batter was looking for and knowing how to throw something different. Robbie was asking Eagle to give each pitch the special touch, that "perfect game" magic.

Wrango had been whamming low strikes against the Colts, but he didn't wham this one. He fanned it.

This gave Eagle a surge of confidence. His

next pitch, a crossfire curve, was sharp and extremely fast. It was a brilliant pitch. Wrango's quick wrists whipped the bat at the ball, but he only managed to nick it foul. Robbie heard the foul tip buzz past his ear.

Eagle's next two pitches were masterpieces of junk. The first waste pitch was a delicious-looking slow curve that was just too far outside for Wrango's taste. Then came a neck-high sailer. But Wrango, who had a keen eye, didn't bite.

Robbie called time and ran out to Eagle.

"What? What?" Eagle asked.

"I want you to take it to this guy, Eags. On this pitch. I want your fastest fast ball. Okay?"

Eagle had been looking at Robbie doubtfully. But as Robbie talked, Eagle got into the idea. "You're on, Robbie!" Eagle said, his eyes lighting up. "You got it!" He turned and started rubbing the ball up.

Robbie ran back to his position. He signaled for the fast ball to let the infielders know what was coming. Sidney Fisher picked up every sign Robbie gave, and relayed it to the other fielders with his own system of signals.

Usually, Eagle sent his fast ball over the plate corners. This one he sent right toward the middle. Because he was throwing it with all his might, the margin of error was bigger. The pitch did something that surprised Robbie. As Eagle released the ball, it looked as if it were moving at an average speed. But as the ball drew closer, it seemed to accelerate. Wrango swung late and hit air. The mighty Wrango had struck out!

Robbie wanted to see just how bad a pitch the next batter, Jim Stretch, would swing at. Eagle's crossfire change-up floated a full foot outside the plate—and Stretch still swung at it! He made contact somehow, and the ball squibbed down to Jeff Streets at first base for the second out.

"All right, Eagle!" said Robbie as the infield threw the ball around crisply. "Just perfect!"

Robbie remembered that Jefferson Pound had trouble with the splitter. But Eagle didn't throw that pitch. The closest thing he had was an overhand curve that broke down. But it didn't have the speed and surprise of the splitter. Robbie didn't know what to call against Jefferson Pound.

Then Robbie heard a familiar voice call from the seats behind the Redstone dugout. "Let's see some more of that smoke, Robbie boy!"

It was the voice of Eddie Trent, the New York Titans' all-star catcher! Robbie looked over briefly and saw Eddie wave at him. *What's Eddie Trent doing here?* Robbie wondered. But Robbie heard what Eddie had called out. Eddie had just told Robbie to get Eagle to throw that same challenging fast ball to Jefferson Pound. Robbie gave the fast-ball sign and followed it with a shaking fist, as if saying, "Throw it even harder than before!"

Again, the ball seemed to start out lazily, then zoomed suddenly at the last moment. Pound swung late and missed.

"Ump," said Pound, turning a pleasant face toward the umpire, "could you check the ball to see if he installed little rockets in it before that pitch?"

"You mean a spitball, son?" asked the umpire, not amused.

"No, sir. Sorry. I was just joking."

"Funny time to be funny," said the umpire.

Robbie knew this umpire was a serious sort, so he didn't say anything. Robbie called for a cutter fast ball close off the inside corner. Pound let it go, but the umpire called it a strike!

"Great pitch, Eags!" Robbie said, snapping the ball back to him. *A little inside, but a great pitch at the right moment!* he thought.

Eagle reached back and threw another zooming fast ball. Pound trickled it down toward Tip Tyree at third base. The ball bounced smooth and true, but Tip bobbled it, then bobbled it again. He didn't bother to throw to first base. Pound was safe on an error.

Robbie saw Eagle's shoulders begin to slump. "All right, Eags, great pitching and a bad break!" shouted Robbie. "Be cool down there, Tip! It's all right. Forget it!"

All the Colts shouted encouragement to Tip.

153

even Eagle. The team wouldn't be broken by an error. Errors happen.

Eagle mowed the next batter down on three straight strikes. The last strike was the zooming fast ball Eddie Trent liked so much. Eagle hadn't stopped his "perfect" pitching just because an error had marred it.

As the Colts ran into the dugout for their at-bats in the bottom of the fourth inning, Robbie felt a rush of pride. *This is a whole team now*, he thought. Robbie felt honored to be part of it no matter how the game turned out.

The Colts scratched out another run in the bottom of the fourth inning. Tip Tyree walked, and Sidney Fisher put a perfect bunt down the first-base line. Wrango wanted the bunt to roll foul so badly that he started blowing on it. The ball stayed fair, however, and Sid was on first base with a bunt single.

With runners on first and second and no outs, Eagle Wilson stepped up to the plate. On the first pitch, he surprised everyone—himself included—by knocking a ground-ball single between first and second base. Tip Tyree scored on the hit. Redstone trailed Skyler by 5–3.

No other runs were scored by the Colts that inning, but their spirit soared as they took the field again. Slowly but surely, they were creeping back into the game.

Eagle pitched another three innings of almost

perfect ball. Robbie admired the gritty determination he showed. Skyler's "Bermuda Triangle" went down meekly in the top of the seventh inning—two strikeouts and an infield pop-up.

Trouble was, Buzz Petroff regained some of the confidence he lost earlier. He matched Eagle's scoreless pitching over the same three innings. So the score remained 5–3 as the game entered the eighth inning.

Warming up, Eagle suddenly winced. This time, Robbie could see Eagle was not faking it. He was in serious pain. Time was called as Redstone's trainer hurried out to the mound. Eagle couldn't lift his arm above his head. The trainer escorted him to the dugout and packed his arm in ice. But even from the bench, trying to fight off the pain, Eagle shouted support to his teammates.

Standing near the dugout, Robbie told Brian and Joshua about Eddie Trent being in the stands. Brian mentioned to Robbie that Eddie was to give out the awards after the game.

The Titan star had recently undergone minor knee surgery. But Eddie had recovered enough to make it to today's game. His Titans were playing in a nearby city that evening. Eddie would take a short flight to the game after this college regional final. It was expected that Eddie Trent would be on the disabled list for two more weeks.

But it was still early in the major-league season. Eddie would have plenty of games to make up for lost time. And right now, he was finding plenty of inspiration watching the Colts fight back.

Coach Frank Preston signaled to the bullpen for Roger Conklin. As Roger jogged toward the mound from the outfield, the Skyler batter muttered, "Who's the dweeb?"

Robbie heard it and went out to the mound to meet Roger. Coach Preston was there, too.

"Here's the ball, Roger," said Frank Preston, handing it over. "You know what to do with it. Three up, three down. Okay?"

Roger nodded, and Coach Preston returned to the dugout.

"Uh, Rog, I don't know how I should say this," began Robbie, "but—"

"But what? Spit it out!" Roger was all business.

"That Bear batter"—here, Robbie peered behind him toward home plate—"called you a dweeb."

"Dweeb, huh?" said Roger, picking up the rosin bag and slamming it down. "Well, this is one dweeb he'll hit nothing but air on!"

Robbie turned and went back to his position behind home plate.

"What are you smiling at, catcher?" asked the Bear batter, seeing the grin on Robbie's face.

"Oh, nothing," said Robbie, squatting. "Nothing at all."

Three blazing fast balls came in, followed by three swings and three misses. This first out was duplicated twice more. Roger Conklin had struck out the side on nine pitches—all heat!

Oscar Gonzales led off the bottom of the eighth inning with a line-drive single to center field. Then Buzz Petroff's tiredness started to show. Using Robbie's lighter bat, Hank Greengrass whacked a fast ball for a single to left field. Wally Potenza followed with a walk to load the bases.

Now Robbie was up. The bases were loaded, there were no outs, and his team was down by two runs. Robbie wanted a home run so badly he could almost taste it.

But he had to cool his heels because the Bears were bringing in their relief ace, Jo Jo Rubens. Jo Jo pitched with a whippy underhand delivery. His fast ball averaged in the high eighties. The underhand delivery gave it a large, bending hop.

Robbie took a look at the first whippy fast ball for a called strike. The next one looked just like the first. But as Robbie started to swing, the ball started curving. He adjusted his wrists to a different angle as he swung, and smacked the pitch deep to left field. The Bears' left fielder, Jefferson Pound, faded back, back, back ... and caught it against the wall! Oscar tagged up from third base and scored easily. Sacrifice fly! The score was now 5–4. There was only one out, with runners on first and second.

Robbie's teammates congratulated him heartily as he came back into the dugout. He felt glad about knocking in the run, but also a little disappointed he hadn't knocked in more runs.

Jeff Streets struck out, making it two outs now. Would the Colts fail to take better advantage of this rally?

That's when the "Lone Ranger," as Lou Ranger was sometimes called, came to the rescue! He crashed a single, tying the score, 5–5. Redstone fans yelled and whooped with excitement. There were runners on first and second now, and two outs. Tip Tyree was up. Everyone in the Colts' dugout was on the top step, clapping and hollering encouragement to him.

"Come on, Tip!" Robbie called. "You can do it!"

"Come on, Tippy, just a single!" yelled Eagle at the top of his lungs.

Tip cracked a one-bouncer between shortstop and third base. The Skyler shortstop went all out for it. But he couldn't get it. Wally Potenza tore around third as Frank Preston waved him home. Wally fell into a beautiful hook slide on the outside of the line. The Bears' catcher took the throw and swept the tag toward Wally's sliding leg. But Wally's toe ticked the plate right before the tag! The Colts were now ahead, 6–5!

They had come back and taken their first lead of the game!

Sidney Fisher flied out to end the inning. Now all the Colts had to do was retire the eighth, ninth, and leadoff batters for the Bears—and the game was theirs.

But Roger Conklin couldn't find the plate. His usually wonderful control deserted him. A single, hit batter, and walk loaded the bases. And the "Bermuda Triangle" were the next three batters.

Frank replaced Roger Conklin with his junk-ball-throwing brother, Wyatt. Wyatt's control was not always reliable, but the Redstone manager had no choice. Robbie took a long time in a huddle with Wyatt before play resumed. He wanted to give him time to get used to everything.

For Pete Wrango, Robbie called a lot of low, sinking junk balls. Two of Wyatt's knucklers veered into the dirt, and Robbie made good stops of these potential wild pitches. Robbie couldn't afford to let one of Wyatt's unpredictable pitches get by him with the bases loaded.

Wrango finally hit a knee-high sinker hard on the ground to Sid Fisher at second base. Sid fielded the ball perfectly and fired it to Robbie. Robbie stretched for the throw like a first baseman. His right foot remained on the plate as he caught Sid's throw for the force-out at home. Robbie quickly got rid of the ball to Jeff Streets, stretching from first. Out! Double play! No score!

There were two outs now. Robbie was very eager to get Jim Stretch out. The Colts' catcher wanted the game to end *before* Jefferson Pound got up. Wyatt's junk balls were perfect for the kind of exaggerated bad pitches Robbie wanted to tempt Stretch with. The only problem was that there were men on second and third. If the ball got by Robbie, the tying run and maybe the winning run would score. But Robbie had confidence in his ability to block pitches.

After the first one, he wasn't so sure. The knuckling curve ball sailed way to the right, a foot away from Stretch's swing. Robbie leapt sideways in a full dive. He barely caught the ball. The Bear runners stayed put, and Wyatt had a strike on Stretch.

Wyatt's next pitch was even more ridiculous, yet Stretch swung at it as well! It was a screwball that nearly hit his back foot. Stretch complained that the ball hit his shoe. The umpire examined the ball and found no shoe polish on it. Strike two!

With an 0–2 count on him, Stretch could expect some waste pitches. But Stretch had already been thrown *two* waste pitches! Robbie thought, *Since he's expecting another ridiculous fishball, he may not be ready for something different.* Robbie signaled for a fast ball down the middle.

So far, Redstone's pitchers had thrown almost

nothing but waste pitches to Stretch. This would be the biggest surprise of all.

Wyatt took the signal in stride, giving away nothing. He normally had a fast ball that clocked below eighty miles per hour. But he threw this one around ninety. Robbie had never seen a faster pitch from Wyatt!

Stretch *was* taken by surprise, but he managed to recover and chop at the ball. It was a foul tip that bounced off the top of Robbie's helmet and rose about ten feet behind him.

Robbie's ears were ringing, but he turned around like a cat and ran after the foul ball still airborne. *Get it! Get it!* he kept telling himself silently. His spikes bit into the dirt. His mask was still on. He didn't think he had the split second it took to fling the mask off. He dove headfirst. His mitt stretched straight out in front of him.

Sliding on his chest protector, Robbie stretched as he had never stretched before. The ball floated into the top of his webbing, bobbed up briefly, then nestled into it. He closed his mitt around the ball.

Redstone fans went wild. Their team had done it! The Colts had come back from a 5–0 deficit to win the regional tournament championship! They would now go on to the College World Series!

And we did it as a team! thought Robbie, still lying on his belly.

Chapter Fifteen

After the game, microphones were put up around home plate. The two teams stood on either side of them. In the awards ceremony, a number of men and women gave short speeches of praise for all the people involved in the regional tournament.

Robbie felt great. He had caught Cynthia's eye earlier, and he could tell she was very proud of him. The team looked great. Eagle was talking happily with Wally. Joshua and Brian were clowning around.

And Gus Greengrass had shaken his son's hand proudly. Robbie watched the two talk, and knew Hank was admitting to his dad that he had used a lighter bat. Gus thought for a few seconds, then nodded. They talked some more. To Robbie, it looked as if they were on good terms again.

Robbie was also very aware of how miserable

the Bears felt, and he tried to respect their feelings. The two teams had shaken hands while the mikes were being put up.

The head of the regional tournament made a short speech about what a great baseball game it was. He congratulated all the players. Then he introduced Eddie Trent. The entire stadium stood up and gave Eddie a standing ovation.

Eddie said a few words praising the Skyler Bears. Then he gave the trophy for runner-up to the Bears' co-captains, Jim Stretch and Jefferson Pound. There was a strong round of applause for the Skyler team.

Next, Eddie picked up the trophy for the winning team, and the Colts' fans stood and cheered. Eddie talked about the grit the Colts had shown in coming back, one of the toughest things to do in baseball. He praised their teamwork and the efforts of all their pitchers. He also praised Tip Tyree's clutch single that scored the winning run.

Robbie couldn't help but notice that Eddie hadn't mentioned him yet. *That's okay*, thought Robbie. But underneath, he was wishing he had done more with that bases-loaded situation than hit a sacrifice fly.

To ringing applause, Eddie handed the winning team's trophy to Redstone's captain, Oscar Gonzales. Oscar held it high for a final round of applause. It was loud and long.

Then Eddie picked up a smaller trophy. "There's one other trophy to be given out," he said. His voice rang out clear even with the echoes from the loudspeakers. "The panel of judges for this regional tournament has chosen the winner of the Most Valuable Player Award. This trophy goes to the player in the tournament who contributed the most to his team.

"I'm personally very happy to be here today to give this award, for I know the young man who's won it."

Uh-oh, thought Robbie.

"This year's MVP hit an amazing .623 during the tournament! And the sacrifice fly he hit in the eighth inning drove in his one-hundredth run for the season!"

At this point, the crowd burst into applause. Robbie blushed.

"He also contributed incredible catching, with no passed balls. And he has an arm so strong that I'm starting to feel the winds of youth breathe down my neck!"

The crowd laughed and gave Eddie a large hand.

"What he gave today was nothing less than his all. He did everything he could to help his team to victory. And for that especially, I am proud to present this year's Most Valuable Player Award to the Redstone Colts' catcher, Robbie Belmont!"

There was a tremendous ovation. People in the stands and all those down on the field were applauding Robbie. He waved to his mother and father in the stands, then to Cynthia. Robbie walked up to where Eddie Trent was standing by the microphones and shook his hand. Eddie patted him on the back. The crowd clapped louder. "Here, Robbie," said Eddie, moving away from the microphones, "say something."

All of a sudden, Robbie's mouth got dry and his knees started to shake. He thought, *Talk? Me? I? Say something? Here? Right now?* But what he said was, "Thanks, Eddie."

Robbie stood in front of the microphones. The applause got louder for a bit, then faded to nothing. Robbie began in a low voice. The words tumbled out. "FirstofallI'dliketothank—"

He stopped. He had to remind himself not to talk too fast. *This is just as hard as baseball!* he thought.

Robbie started again. "First of all, I'd like to thank the Skyler University Bears for the great game they gave us today. Next, I want to thank all my teammates. Without their play, their support, I wouldn't be speaking to you now. And I want to thank Frank Preston for his great . . . managering."

Here, both the crowd and his teammates laughed at Robbie's made-up word. Even Coach

Preston and his staff were beaming. Robbie felt they were all behind him, *for* him.

"I also want to thank Eddie Trent and all my friends here today, all the tournament officials, and all of *you* for making it such a pleasure to play this game.

"But I especially want to thank my mother and my father. They never doubted me when I sometimes even doubted myself. Mom, Dad"—Robbie held up his trophy for them—"thank you for this and so much more!"

The crowd broke into warm applause as Robbie held his trophy in the air. When he lowered it, he saw what was engraved on the gold rectangle at the base of the trophy:

Division One College Regionals
MVP

Soon, a third line would be engraved:

Robbie Belmont

167

Behind the Iron Mask

Great baseball action and off-field drama await you in all six of Gary Carter's Iron Mask books. Future Hall of Famer Gary Carter, a ten-time National League selection as catcher for the annual All-Star Game and the 1984 All-Star Game MVP, has closely consulted on this baseball series. And he has written a personal introduction for each book. Follow the exciting exploits of Iron Mask series' hero Robbie Belmont as he rises from high-school star...to college record breaker...to promising pro!